SHADOWS ON OUR SKIN

Jennifer Johnston is accepted as one of the finest Irish writers and has an international reputation. Her other books include *The Gates, How Many Miles to Babylon?, The Old Jest*, winner of the 1979 Whitbread Award for Fiction, *The Christmas Tree, The Railway Station Man, Fool's Sanctuary, The Captains and the Kings* and *The Invisible Worm*. Many of her books are published by Penguin. Jennifer Johnston lives in Northern Ireland.

Shadows on Our Skin was shortlisted for the 1977 Booker Prize.

SHADOWS ON OUR SKIN

JENNIFER JOHNSTON

PENGUIN BOOKS

For B. Friel with constant admiration

PENGUIN BOOKS

Published by the Penguin Group
Penguin Books Ltd, 27 Wrights Lane, London W8 5TZ, England
Penguin Books USA Inc., 375 Hudson Street, New York, New York 10014, USA
Penguin Books Australia Ltd, Ringwood, Victoria, Australia
Penguin Books Canada Ltd, 10 Alcorn Avenue, Toronto, Ontario, Canada M4V 3B2
Penguin Books (NZ) Ltd, 182–190 Wairau Road, Auckland 10, New Zealand

Penguin Books Ltd, Registered Offices: Harmondsworth, Middlesex, England

First published by Hamish Hamilton 1977
Published in Penguin Books 1991
5 7 9 10 8 6

The author acknowledges assistance from
the Arts Council of Great Britain

Printed in England by Clays Ltd, St Ives plc

I see the last black swan
Fly past the sun.
I wish I, too, were gone
Back home again.

Now we've got time to kill'
Kill the shadows on our skin.
Kill the fire that burns within.
Killing time my friend.

My body's black and sore.
I need to sleep.
Now hear the heaven's roar.
I can't escape.

With acknowledgments and thanks to Horslips.

Father, you had to go away.
And sadly I have had to stay.
I am sad we had to part.
I will miss you in my heart.

He chewed the end of his pen and tried to visualise the words printed in the *Journal*, even perhaps with the importance of a thick black line around them, presenting them to the world. No, anyway. He crossed them out, carefully inking out each word so that no one would be able to read it.

Dear father I am sad you had to go.
So, blow, flow, po . . . ha ha . . . slow, oh, oh, oh.
Miss McCabe's chalk squealed pitifully on the blackboard. A triangle. Three sides. A.B.C. Three angles. Triangle.
He saw his father propped against grey pillows, his head folded down into his shoulders like some ancient bird.

Father, it's time for you to go,
But don't think my tears will flow,
Because I hate you so.

His fingers trembled as he wrote the word hate.
The sides of the triangle are all the same length. Squeak. A to B. Squeak. B to C. C to A. An equilateral triangle. All equal.

Your eyes are blue,
Your nose is red,
I wish that you were bloody dead.

That means that each angle must be 60 degrees. Angle A,
60 degrees. Angle B 60 degrees. Angle C 60 degrees. Thus
making 180 degrees.

You've lived too long, already, Dad.
And when you go I won't be sad.
I'll jump for joy and shout and sing,
Dee da dee da dee da dee ding.

Now hands up those who can tell me the name of a
triangle with three sides the same length. Martin Casey.
That's right. An equilateral triangle. EQUILATERAL. Squeak,
squeak.

When you go to the heavenly land
I'll hang out the flags and order the band.

That, now, had a ring about it. A kind of dancing rhythm.
What degrees are the angles of an equilateral triangle?
Joseph Logan?

The drums will beat
And the bells will ring . . .
'Joseph Logan.'
A terrible silence filled the room and then he heard his
name spoken once more.
'Joseph Logan.'
'Yes, miss?'
'Thank you for your attention.'
A murmur of sycophantic laughter.
She pointed with the chalk to the lines on the board.
'What degree is angle A?'
'Er . . .'

8

'Angle B?'

'Well . . .'

'I suppose it is too much to expect you to know what angle C is. What angle C must be?'

'I'm sorry, miss . . .'

She spread her hands out towards the rest of the class, who roared in one triumphant voice, '60 degrees, miss.'

She wrote 60 degrees on the board and then turned to face Joseph again.

'What do you call this particular triangle, Joseph?'

He looked past her at the board.

'Equ . . .' he read. 'Equ . . .' He left it at that. There was no point in getting tangled up in the other letters. He knew they wouldn't sound the way they looked.

'Equilateral,' said Miss McCabe. Her mouth was angry. She underlined the word three times and then the chalk broke. She threw the pieces on to her desk.

'I am here to teach, Joseph,' she said. 'You are here to learn. The law,' she spoke the word with contempt,' demands that you attend school. If I had my way I would open that door, and let you and all the others who don't wish to learn go home and wallow in your ignorance. Wallow.'

She opened her desk and took out a new piece of chalk.

'One day, when it is too late you will regret your inattention. Regret this incredible waste of time. Your time and, I may say, my time. You will remain behind after the others have gone home.' She sighed and turned towards the board. The class sighed too, they had hoped for better things.

By the time Joe was let out of school the town was beginning to lose its colour. The rows of houses up the hill behind had the look of cardboard cut-outs against the draining sky. The wind that blew up the valley was cold and the day's dust and several crisp bags played dismally around Joe's feet as he walked along the road. He was in no hurry to get home. Mam never got back from the café much before

9

a quarter to six and it was more than likely that the old fella'd be sending him out on messages here, there and everywhere, and Mam would catch him at it and there would be ructions. More ructions. It was that sort of day. A ructious day. There weren't many people about. Down below him in the distance a couple of shots were fired and then there was silence. The street lamps were flowering and people had not yet drawn their curtains, so the dusk glittered. He stopped by a long low wall and put his school bag down on it. His mother hated him to loiter. He shoved his clenched fists into the pockets of his anorak and huddled it around him, against the wind. A mist of smoke from the thousands of houses below drifted along the valley. The only colour to be seen now was the green grass of the hill across the valley, on top of which rose the grey walls that surrounded the city. A seagull drifted on the wind, out too late for safety. It was being blown away from the river back towards the hills. With an effort it moved its wings and turned steeply, setting off for home again. Joe picked up his school bag and took the hint. He passed a couple of shops, the windows barricaded, with stripes of light between the planks, 'Business as usual' scrawled on the closed doors. He turned off the main road down the hill, past a row of derelict cottages, the windows frightening holes. He began to run. This stretch of the road always put fear in him. Around the corner a couple of men were strolling casually. Joe slowed his feet. He always felt that to run for no good reason made other people nervous. One of the men laughed at some joke. Joe sauntered past them.

'Isn't it Joe Logan?'

'Yes,' said Joe.

They all stopped walking and looked at each other. The taller of the two men was chewing gum.

'Time you were home,' he commented.

The other man scratched his nose with a very long finger.

'How's your old man?'

Joe shrugged slightly.

'He's O.K.'

'Just the same bloody old bastard as usual.'

'Sssh,' said the gum chewer.

'That's about it.' He felt elevated by the casualness of his answer.

The two men laughed. Joe laughed.

'Any news from Brendan?'

'Mam gets letters . . .'

The men were bored.

'Time you were home anyway.'

The wail of a fire engine, or perhaps an ambulance. Joe turned his head to see if he could see anything through the broken houses. There were some more shots from the other side of the valley.

'Get on home.'

When Joe turned to look at the two men there was no longer anyone there. They had been, maybe, a figment of his imagination.

The moment he opened the door he heard the voice calling him.

'Joe.'

He hung his coat up and went into the kitchen.

The drums will beat and the bells will ring.

'Joe.'

The stove would be out if he didn't put something on it soon.

She always left a scuttle of anthracite by the stove. He put his school bag down on the table.

'Joe.' And then a fit of coughing, great deep, gut-splintering coughs. He took the top-plate off the stove and lifted the scuttle. Batter, batter, batter, over and above the coughing. It was the sound of the stick on the floor above. The ultimate summons. A good blackthorn that had belonged to his father before him. Then the clatter of fuel into the almost empty stove. He put the scuttle down on the floor again and opened the damper to get a bit of heat up before she came in.

'I'm coming,' he answered at last, but the battering continued until his hand was on the bedroom door knob.

His father was lying on top of the bed fully dressed but for his shoes, which lay empty on the floor. He had a blanket pulled over him for warmth. The room smelt of sweat and beer and sickness. It had always smelt the same as long as Joe could remember. One bar of an electric fire burned up what good air there was and gave out a little warmth in return. A saucer full of butts and a dirty glass were on the table beside the bed and a pile of newspapers were tumbled on the floor. The grey man on the bed looked at his son with anger.

'What kept you?'

'Nothing kept me.'

'You should have been home by four. Where were you? I'm parched.'

There was a long silence while son looked at father and father closed his eyes to indicate his incapacity.

'Did you not go down at all today then?' asked the boy.

'How could I? I got this pain round my heart the moment your Mammy left the house. I was only able to stoop down and strip off my shoes. I thought I was gone that time.'

I'll hang out the flags and order the band.

'It's not right she should leave me like that.'

The eyes opened to cunning slits, gauging, biding, then a little more they parted to show misty pupils surrounded by a web of red streaks. Mucus pulled at the corners.

'I'm parched,' he whined again.

'Mammy'll be in soon. I'll make you a cup of tea.'

'I could do better with a couple of bottles of stout.'

He groped under his pillows and pulled out a pound note. He held it out towards Joe.

'Here.'

'What's that?'

'Don't you know bloody well what it is? Here. Take it and

12

get on away round to McMonagles and get me a couple of Guinness and a packet of fags.'

'Ah, Dad . . .'

'Ah, Dad yourself to hell out of here.'

'They're shooting.'

'What's that to do with you if they're shooting. They're not going to be wasting their bullets on you. Here.'

He waved the note with remarkable vigour for one so ill.

'Where did you get that money anyway?'

'That's none of your bloody business. Here. Here. Take the money and get out of this before she comes in.'

Joe took the money from his father's thin fingers and stood looking at it. The man on the bed looked relieved. He pulled the blanket up around his shoulders and shoved his head down deeper into the pillows.

'That's a good lad, and lookit, before you go, I'm perished, shove on the other bar of the fire.'

Joe went over to the fire and pressed down the metal switch.

Crackle went the end of the element. A star sparked and went out. There was a smell of burning dust. Joe ran out of the room and down the stairs. Behind him the lung rattling coughs began once more.

'And get a move on.' The voice that followed him down the stairs wasn't too feeble.

The wind had brought sleet, which danced in and out of the lamplight. The curtains were all pulled now and through occasional cracks you could see the sparkle of the tellies. The shooting seemed quite near suddenly, and from round the corner came the sound of glass breaking. Joe hesitated and then his mother appeared, her head bent forward against the sleet, her legs pumping her up the hill.

Ructions. He stood back into a doorway, hoping that she would pass by without seeing him. Down at the bottom of the hill a crowd of boys were shouting.

'I see you,' her voice said. 'Skulking, that's what you're doing. Skulking.'

13

He stepped out into the light.

'It's only ostriches put their heads in the sand and think they can't be seen. It's no kind of a night to be out, son. I bet I know the nature of your business.'

She held her hand out towards him. With a certain guilt and a certain pleasure he took the pound from his pocket and gave it to her. She snapped it angrily into her bag.

'Hurry,' she said. 'Come on, hurry. They're up to something tonight.'

Inside the door she shook the drops from her coat and hung it up. She held out her hand for Joe's anorak.

'Is that you back, Joe?'

'No. It's me back.'

There was silence for a moment and then a creaking of bedsprings and two thuds as his feet hit the floor.

'Don't disturb yourself.' She only spoke the words in a half-whisper as she walked down the passage into the kitchen. They could hear his uncertain steps above them. She filled the kettle and put it on the stove.

'Have you much homework?'

'Not much. I'll do it after tea.'

'You might as well start it now and not be wasting time.'

Feet clumbered on the stairs. There were pauses for coughing between each step. She busied herself, wiping at things with a cloth, getting out the pan, her hands nervously flying here and there. Joe took some books out of his bag and sat down at the end of the table.

Meisse agus Pangur Bán,
Cechtar nathar fria shaindán,
Bíthamenma-sam fri seilgg
Mo menma céinin shaincheird.

He mouthed the words silently. He saw in his head, the old monk and the white cat, their heads nodding slightly as people's heads did in concentration. The pan hissed with heating fat. The door opened.

'Is my tea ready yet?'

14

'Amn't I only in this minute. I haven't even taken off my wet shoes.'

'The boy was late from school.'

He struggled across the room and lowered himself into the chair at the other end of the table.

'What kept you, son?'

As she spoke, she peeled strips of streaky bacon off the top of the pile and laid them with great care on the pan.

'I was kept back by the teacher.'

'For insubordination? What? Was it that? Rebellion? What? Have we spawned a rebel? Taking after your father? what?'

'Will you leave the boy alone. Can't you see he's doing his homework. The only thing you ever rebelled against was work . . .'

'Always the witty word. Your mother always has the witty word.'

'Meisse agus Pangur Bán,' said Joe aloud, in desperation.

'What's that you're saying?'

'I'm learning my homework.'

'What was it you said but?'

'Meisse agus Pangur Bán,' repeated Joe.

Frying bacon filled the room with its comfortable smell.

'Go on,' The man leant over the table towards him with a small show of enthusiasm.' The next line. I had the Irish once.'

'Cechtar nathar fria shaindán.'

'Yes.'

'Bítha . . .'

'Bítha . . .'

'I forget. I'm only learning it.'

'You'd want to put a bit more work into it.'

'I'm doing it now.'

He ducked his head back towards the book again.

'Aye.' He leaned back in his chair again. His remembering face was softer than the anger of his everyday one. 'I had a bit of the Irish once.'

'Back when you ran the Movement, I suppose.'

She flipped the bacon over on the pan with a knife, and then pushed the slices to one side to make room for the sausages.

'The sarcasm.'

'Aye,' she said. 'That would be right. Sarcasm.'

'Did you get the fags for me?' He spoke to Joe across the table. Without lifting his eyes from the book, Joe shook his head.

'He did not. I met him out in the street and brought him home. You've no call to be sending him out on a night like this. It's a dirty night, and they're shooting.'

'They'll not shoot Joe.'

'Have you never heard of stray bullets? Anyway, he's not going out tonight.'

'I suppose you took the money?'

'Ay. I did.' The only sound for a long time then was the spitting fat in the pan and a slight hum from the kettle.

Meisse agus . . .

Worms of hunger crept in Joe's stomach.

The old man scraped his chair on the ground.

'I'll just have to go up to the shop and get . . .'

'I thought you were next thing to death.'

'. . . some fags.'

He began to heave himself up from the table.

'I'll not be many minutes.'

'I had a letter from Brendan.'

He sat down again. He pushed his red hands out in front of him on the table and looked at them for a moment.

'You did?'

'I did.' She turned round from the stove and patted her pocket. The letter crackled.

'Well?' he asked. His hands were puffy with disuse. His nails bent over the tops of his fingers, ridged and brown.

'Is he well? What does he say?'

'He wants to come home.'

The hands moved apart and then together again and were

16

still, two rather unpleasant animals on the cloth.

Pangur Bán.

White cat watching the mouse hole, breath gathered for springing.

'Ah.' It was a waiting sound.

She went to the cupboard and took out a bowl of eggs.

'Is that all you're going to say?'

'I don't know what to say.'

'At a loss for words? What is the matter with you at all?'

Cecthar anthar Brendan.

'I've been thinking all day, you must write and tell him not to come.'

Brendan agus Pangur.

'Wouldn't it be great to have him back.'

The hands danced slowly for a moment.

'It would be great altogether.'

She broke an egg into the pan and scooped the bubbling fat over it. It spat, reflecting her own anger. She dodged her head sideways a little to avoid the stinging fat.

'I don't want him back.'

Another egg slid in beside the first.

'I'll not write.'

'Joe, clear your books away like a good boy and put the plates on the table.' She poured water from the kettle into the large metal teapot.

'Brendan . . .' There was almost pleasure in his voice as he said the word.

'Brendan nothing. He's not coming back here if I can help it.'

'Why not?' asked Joe with interest.

The question was ignored.

'I'll not write. You write and tell him that if you want to. Tell him he's not welcome in his own home.'

'It's not that. You know well.'

'I'll not write.'

'You'll write. I don't want him coming back here. He has

a good job over there. He's out of trouble. Do you want him in trouble?'

She turned round from the stove and held out the spoon towards him in a gesture of appeal. Hot fat spotted the floor.

'Can you not see?'

'If Brendan wants to come home we have no right to stop him. I see that.'

'You could advise him. He's been away two years. He doesn't know what it's like here. Advise him. That's all I ask.'

Three forks, three knives, three cups, three plates, butter, jam, salt, milk. Father's hands lay still amongst the cutlery and china. Strange ornaments.

'He's a man.'

Ketchup, pepper, bread.

'I'll not interfere.'

Sugar, gritty crystals in a blue bowl.

'He must judge. Have his own opinion.'

'I'm feared for him. He's not wise.'

'A poor reflection on the way you brought him up.'

She put the tea-pot carefully on a blue-rimmed plate on the table before she spoke.

'We,' she said, her mouth tight and tired. 'We brought him up. I slapped him when he was bold and petted him and tried to tell him what was right and what was wrong. You told him fairy stories about yourself and the Movement. Your flowering youth. Your great days. Hero that you were.'

'You have to tell them something. I told no lies.'

'May God forgive you.'

Abruptly she turned back to her cooking.

Joe watched as his father lifted his hands from the table and covered his face.

'Fairy stories . . .' began the boy and then stopped.

'Lies, you might say. Never mind what he says.' Her voice was as cold as the sleet outside.

The man got up from the table and walked slowly to the

18

door. He didn't say a word. He took his coat down from the hook and pulled it round his shoulders. As he opened the hall door a cutting wind blew down the passage past him. Joe made a gesture towards the table.

'Let him go,' said his mother.

The door slammed.

The next day was dour, there was no wind to blow away the smell of the night's burnings. His mother was scrubbing the step as he left for school. Steam rose gently around her crouching body.

'Mind you come home straight from school,' she said, as he jumped across the wet step on to the pavement. Upstairs the curtains were still pulled across his father's window. He would be snoring up there in his stale unhappy room. When he woke his head would be thick with last night's drink and the webs of his fairy tales.

He managed to get through school without any trouble. The words of his poem were at his tongue's tip when they were needed. He shook his head at his friend Peter when he asked him to go and play after school, remembering her words and the shining water on the step, the shape of her hand fitted around the scrubbing brush.

'She told me to go straight home.'

The boys were filling their pockets with pebbles in case they met any soldiers on their way to wherever they were going.

'What's half an hour?' Peter threw a stone into the air and caught it on the back of his hand.

'No,' said Joe. The back of her hand had been like knotted string.

'Ah, go on.'

'I'd better go home.'

'Suit yourself.'

The boys started throwing stones at each other, without weight behind each flick of the arm, without malice. Joe's wave was unnoticed. She had never really liked him going

19

out to play with other children. She had always wanted him to be there with her when he had been small and Brendan had been out at school. She hadn't been able to go out to work then and he never left her side. He went to the shops with her and to the Church, and stood fidgeting on the pavement while she passed the time of day with a neighbour. Sometimes if the sun was shining and she had finished her work around the house she would take him for a walk up to the park, or down along the quay to look at the boats. She taught him to write, setting him at the kitchen table with a box of coloured pencils and a couple of sheets of paper. 'Emm is for Mammy,' she would say, bending over him to draw a great big M at the top of the page. 'Here now, you do it.' She would leave him with his fingers clumsily pushing the pencil across the paper, and get on with her cleaning and boiling. In his whole life no one else's mother had ever boiled things the way she did. She had needed his company there all the time, not, he had somehow been aware, because she couldn't pass an hour without him, but so that she wouldn't have to be alone with his father. He was some sort of protection for her.

'I have the child,' she used to call up at him, when he shouted down for her to run to the shop for his cigarettes, or to the off-licence for a couple of bottles of stout. Then the old man would have to wait for Brendan to come home. Brendan would do it, Brendan was his boy. Brendan was the great lad. He would run those interminable messages after school to the pub, or the bookie. He would go out and look for him on those evenings when Mammy had finally taken his tea out of the oven and angrily scraped it off the plate and into the bucket. It was Brendan who could coax him home and back upstairs to his bed and would then sit by him listening to the stories, over and over again the same stories, the glorious days, the fairy tales. Brendan knew those names as well as he knew his own: Liam Lynch, Ernie O'Malley, Liam Mellows, Sean Russell, the Joes, the Eamons, the Charles, all heroes, dead heroes, living heroes, men of principle, men of action. Heroes. The world was peopled with heroes, with patrols and flying columns and sad songs that used to drift down through the floor to Joe below, songs about death and traitors and freedom and more heroes.

Then Brendan had gone away, gone over there. It had been a summer afternoon and the windows in the street sparkled.

'I don't want to deliver milk bottles forever, kiddo.' He looked down the hill as he spoke and pinched Joe's shoulder between his first finger and his thumb as if to impress something upon him, Joe wasn't quite sure what. In his other hand he carried the old brown suitcase that had lain on top of the wardrobe as long as Joe could remember, gathering dust.

'Might as well be a bloody cow.'

Mam hadn't come to the door to see him off, and the old man had been in his bed for days.

'I'll come back a millionaire.'

He had walked off down the hill, leaning slightly away from the suitcase as he went.

Dad had been bad for weeks after. Ill, shaking all the time and giving off a terrifying smell of illness that made Joe want to keep away from him. He had put his fist one night through the window in the front room, and Mam had filled the black hole with cardboard which had stayed there for the best part of a year. But things were starting to get bad then and soon they weren't the only people with cardboard in their window.

'Provos rule' was written in large white letters on the gable end of a house. A few days ago the letters had been grey, but someone had brightened them up. It was now the brightest thing about the day. If I had a cat I would call it Pangur Bán. It would sit on the wall with its tail curled tidily round its feet and watch Mrs O'Toole's hens scratching for nothing in her back yard. It would jump through the window in the middle of the night and sleep in the bend of my legs, only Mam would say no. No dirty cats on beds, she would say, and then boil the bedclothes.

There was a girl sitting on the low wall which he regarded more or less as his private property. She had her coat clutched round her and she appeared to be staring at the green slope across the valley, or the walls, or the spire of the Cathedral rising above them all. Or maybe, he thought, as he put his schoolbag down on the wall, she was really only staring at the inside of her head. The world's longest stare, the world's most unrewarding stare. He tucked his anorak under his behind and sat down also. He had seen her there before like himself, loitering rather than doing anything sensible. She always carried a briefcase that weighed her down slightly as she walked, reminding him, in fact, of the departing back of Brendan. Now, her briefcase was on the wall beside her and a red-gloved hand held the edges of her coat together at the throat. She was quite unaware of Joe's arrival, even unaware of the wind that tangled her brown hair, and had changed the colour of her face from the palest cream to a pinched mauve. She sat quite motionless, only the wind lifted and stretched her hair out to one side. Suddenly she took her hand from her collar and pushed it into her pocket. She took out a packet of cigarettes and some matches. She put a cigarette into the corner of her mouth, and then, for some reason, became aware of Joe's presence. She turned and gave him a quick look and held out the packet towards him.

'Have you the habit?' She had a stranger's voice.

He blushed and shook his head.

She put the box away again and lit a match. It struggled with the wind for a moment without success.

'I suppose I shouldn't have asked you really. I should have had more . . . er . . . concern.' She laughed. He could see she enjoyed laughing.

She tried another match, this time defending the flame with a crooked hand. Blue smoke crept up through her fingers.

22

'You have the look of a kid who might have the habit.'

He wondered if that was a compliment or not.

'I tried it once, but I couldn't see what was so great about it.'

'I've seen you here before.'

There was a long pause.

'Yes,' he said eventually. 'I like it here.'

He watched her pulling at the cigarette and the smoke trickling gently from her nose.

'I've seen you too. Here.'

'Long ago people used to gather on the tops of hills to watch battles. That was before battles became . . .' she hesitated a moment . . . 'as . . . all-embracing as they are now.'

'Is that what you're doing? Watching battles?' He wondered if she was some sort of journalist or what.

'Not really. I'm not quite sure what I'm doing. I'm not quite sure why I said that anyway . . . about battles, I mean. And you?'

'I just don't like going home.'

She turned and stared at him.

'Why don't you go and play with the others?'

She nodded off to the right where below them some boys were kicking a ball around a concrete playground.

He shrugged.

'I don't know. Sometimes I do. Sometimes I just don't feel like it.'

The conversation fell apart and lay between them on the wall with his schoolbag and her briefcase. They sat in silence for about fifteen minutes. The rising smoke and the thickening light turned the day into evening. It became impossible to keep out the cold. He got up. She sat on, her hands in her pockets, her shoulders slightly hunched.

He picked up his satchel.

'Goodbye.' He spoke nervously as if their brief conversation had never happened. She didn't answer. He could

23

see by her face that she wasn't there to answer. He waited a moment and then began to walk away.

'Oh, hey. You there,' she called after him. 'Boy with the face.' She laughed again.

He turned and waved, a flip of his hand it was really, as he had seen the older boys do.

'What's your name?'

'Joe. Joseph Logan. Well . . . Joe.'

'Goodbye, Joe. It was nice meeting you.'

His father was up and sitting by the kitchen table when he got home.

'Were you kept in again?'

'No.'

'You took your time then.'

'Aye.'

He opened his schoolbag and spread his books on the table.

'Were you with friends?'

Joe shook his head.

'You can tell me. I'll not let on.' The voice had a whine in it.

'I was alone, Dad. Just alone. Have you done the stove?'

'I'd never tell her anything you told me.'

'Have you?'

'I have not. It's always do this, do that. Why can't she stay at home and do these things herself?'

'You know well.'

He knew it was a mistake the moment he had said the words. He picked up the scuttle and rattled a load of anthracite into the stove, hiding the words with the noise and his business. As he put the scuttle down on the floor again he took a sideways glimpse at his father. His eyes were closed but for a glittering thread of blue, and tears spilled down his cheeks.

'I'm sorry,' muttered the boy. 'I meant nothing. I just spoke off the top of my head.'

'Don't think that I am unaware. Don't think I don't cry

24

in my bed when I think what I have become. I am aware, that's all I say.'

He wiped at his fretful eyes with the back of his hand. 'You . . .'

There was a long silence. Joe stood miserably still. He should rattle the ashes out, but he didn't like to.

'You, in your youth, see me for what I am. But. But, let me tell you one thing . . . young fellow . . . I am not . . .' He emphasised the word with a thump on the table. Then, overcome, somehow, by the physical action, he seemed to lose the drift of what he was saying. Joe touched his books, gathered them into a pile at his end of the table while his father groped through the mists in his mind for the words he wanted.

'. . . unaware,' he said finally with a certain triumph. 'That's all I have to say. And let me tell you, when you cast your aspersions at me, when you point your finger . . .' His voice trailed away. His hands on the table wrestled with each other. After a moment or two Joe sat down and pulled his maths book towards him. With a little bit of luck . . .

'Did you put the kettle on?'

Joe sighed.

'No.'

'I could do with a cup of tea.'

Joe brought the kettle out to the scullery and filled it and put it on the stove.

'I burned myself out. That's what I did. A burned skeleton, that's what I am. No sinew left. No gut. No damn gut. I burned out, son. I bet no boy in your class has seen his father cry. Has he? Has he?'

He opened his eyes wide and fixed them on Joe.

'Has he?' He almost shouted the words.

'I don't know, Dad. Honest, I don't know. We don't talk about that sort of thing.'

'I cry.' He said it in a very matter of fact voice. The tears on his cheeks were dry now, only grey tracks remained.

'I have cried for years. There's been nothing else for me

25

to do. No one understands. No one.' His battling hands lay still. 'Only Brendan. He came near to it. Near. He would listen. Sit there and listen, so he would.'

'To your fairy stories?'

'Your mother has me destroyed with her tongue. She's a bitter woman.'

'Oh,' said Joe.

He took the teapot down from the shelf and poured some hot water into it.

'I was, after all, for a short moment of my life, a hero. That is something. Something, hey, son? Isn't that better than a kick up the backside? Son?'

'Yes, I suppose so.'

'Make it good and strong. I need it strong.'

Joe emptied the water back into the kettle and put three spoonfuls of tea into the pot.

'Once a hero always a hero. True? Would you say that was true?'

The boy poured the boiling water into the teapot and put the lid on. He shook his head.

'I suppose so.'

'Well, you can take it from me it's not true. Not true. There's not a bloody sod in this city would take off his hat to me in the street. Or even pass the time of day. Here, give me that tea.'

'It's not drawn yet.'

'No matter. I want to be away before she comes in.'

He watched while Joe put milk in a mug and then shook the teapot for a moment to mix the leaves round a bit.

'I could die in the night.'

When you go to the heavenly land
I'll hang out the flags and order the band.

The tea spurted out of the spout, colouring the milk and freckling it with a thousand tiny black grains.

'So I could. Die.'

He looked gloomily into the mug, regretting his haste.
'And not a moment too soon.'
He stirred in three large spoons of sugar to give it some taste.
'I should have died then, instead of being mutilated, body and soul. Aye, soul too. I have wasted away my life since.'

The drums will beat,
The bells will ring,
Hail another hero,
The angels will sing.
And I will clap my hands and cheer
Because you are no longer ...

The hand that lifted the cup was trembling so that the tea lurched over the side of the cup and trickled over the fingers down on to the table. With a sudden gesture of rage the man threw the cup on to the floor.
'I can't drink that muck.'
The cup broke neatly into three pieces and the tea spread over the linoleum in thin curves, leaving a pile of leaves and unmelted sugar under the white china segments.
He got slowly to his feet, hands pushing against the edge of the table, feet scraping on the floor.
'Oh God.'
His body had become a dead weight which he dragged across the room and down the passage to the door. Joe stooped down and picked up the broken pieces of china. The sound of the dragging steps, the heavy breath filled his throat and chest with hate.
He was in the scullery wringing out the cloth with which he had wiped the floor when he heard his mother come into the house. The wind rattled the back door. In Mrs O'Toole's yard something was loose and banging gently against the roof of the hen house. He poked the tea leaves down the sink with a finger. She'd eat him for that, if the drain got blocked. He could see her in his mind shaking

27

the drops of rain off her coat and then raising herself on her toes to hang it on the hook by the door. It was her shopping night and she would have plastic bags that would have pained her arms as she carried them up the hill.

'Joe.'

He gave a final swirl to the water in the sink and wiped his hands on his trousers.

'Are you in, Joe?'

Didn't she know well he was in, wasn't his coat hanging there beside hers?

'I'm in.'

He went back into the kitchen. She stood out in the passage looking nervous somehow, as if she had come to the wrong house. He sat down and pulled his books towards him.

'What are you doing?'

'Homework.'

She came into the kitchen with her plastic bags, bending forward with the weight as she walked. She put them on the table, crowding his books together.

'Your Daddy?'

She began to take things out of one of the bags. Baked beans, Daz, Typhoo tea, two small packets, six eggs in a cardboard egg box.

'He's been down?'

'Aye. He's been down.'

'I can smell the smell of him.'

'Yes.'

'Where is he now?'

Her eyes moved for a moment upward towards the ceiling. There was only silence, no sound of the springs moving, the death-rattle cough, the murmuring voice. She crunched the plastic bag in her hands.

'Is he dead? Where is the hero's voice that should be calling my name?'

She laughed.

Half a pound of sausages, a crinkled metal pot scourer,

28

that made your fingers sick to touch, a blue and white carton of milk.

'He went out?'

She stood with a cabbage in her left hand looking for all the world like a picture of Victoria Regina that Joe had seen in a book somewhere.

'Out,' he repeated foolishly.

'What did you let him go out for?'

'How could I stop him?'

She nodded abruptly and put the cabbage on the table.

'How indeed,' was all she said.

She let him get on with his work then. She laid the table just for the two of them.

His father didn't come in until after he had gone to bed.

He never pulled his curtains at night, but liked to lie in his bed by the window staring out at the changing sky. There had been two explosions and the darkness was coloured by glowing smoke which rose beyond the wet roofs of the other side of the street. He heard the fire engines and the ambulances, the distant sounds of shouting voices. He was warm and his eyes drooped gently into darkness. The smell of burning crept even through the closed window. People laughed below in the street. People always managed to laugh. What's the joke, fellas? The house trembled as a helicopter rattled over the roofs, the searchlight probing, searching. He wondered if they had X-ray gadgets that could see through brick walls and drawn curtains, see him curled in his bed, see his waiting mother pressing the iron heavily down on the steaming shirts. Even into the blackness of people's skulls. All things are possible. What does a thought look like? What shape? What substance? Like an equilateral triangle perhaps? He smiled as he tumbled down into warm thoughtless darkness. His thoughts were like birds, there untouchable in front of him, skiting away as he tried to trap them, in a whirl of feathers, and then appearing again, dipping and soaring across the sky of his mind.

He was awakened by the sound of their voices quarrelling below. The impotent unhappy sound of it stripped him of his warmth. It was inescapable, the sound of it, like the stinging smell of smoke that lay night and day around the city.

The girl was sitting on the wall again the next afternoon. The sun was shining, but it didn't appear to have any effect on the temperature. Tired dust rose from the streets and lay again on the grass and trees.

'Hallo, Joe Logan.' She smiled as he approached.

'Hallo.'

He had been intending to go straight home, but he paused.

'Are you sitting today? It's a better day for sitting than yesterday.'

She patted the wall beside her with a hand.

He must have looked dubious, because she grinned.

'I won't eat you.'

What did she think he was anyway, a mere kid?

'Or abduct you. Or . . . anything.'

A kid.

'My name's Kathleen.'

She folded her hands neatly on her knee and began to recite.

'Kathleen Doherty is my name,

Ireland is my nation.

Derry, referred to by some as Londonderry, is my dwelling place.

And heaven, my destination.'

'Expectation,' he corrected her, and put his schoolbag on the wall beside hers.

'Ah,' she said. 'It's as well to know where you're going. It gives you a feeling of security.'

'No one ever knows that they're going to heaven till they get there.'

She looked vaguely across at the Cathedral with a slight smile on her face.

'So they tell you anyway,' he insisted. 'They should know.'

He sat down on the wall.

'Shouldn't they?'

She spread her two hands out towards him. They were still red-gloved, with dark winding patterns round each finger.

'How can they know? How can anyone know? Do you really think that God whispers some secret in their ears. Their ears only? Baa baa black sheep, that's all they say to us.'

He was alarmed for a moment, then she laughed, suddenly and vigorously.

'Anyway,' she said, when she had finished laughing. 'It's a daft sort of way to start a conversation.'

He agreed in his head.

'There's a lot of Dohertys around.'

'There are.'

'My Mammy's name was Doherty.'

'Oh.'

'Perhaps we're cousins.'

'I shouldn't think so.'

She began the eternal search for her cigarettes. She didn't seem to have any. She pulled off her gloves impatiently as if they were to blame and searched again.

'Oh damn.'

'What?'

'Out of poison.'

'Poison? Oh yes . . .'

'I'm sure I had a full packet. I'm coming slowly to the conclusion, Joe, that there's a cigarette rustler in the staff room. Or else I'm smoking in my sleep.'

'Are you a teacher?'

'Mmmm.'

'What do you teach?' He couldn't somehow see her coming to grips with the equilateral triangle.

'English . . . at least that's what I'm supposed to teach.

In fact I find myself spouting out whatever happens to be in my mind that day. Do you know what is a past participle?'

'No.'

'Or a semi-colon?'

'No.'

'Or why you mustn't split an infinitive?'

'No. No. No.'

'Neither do I. Nor do I think it matters very much. Unfortunately there are those who do. So.'

There was a very long silence.

'So?' he asked eventually.

'So I don't suppose my career as a teacher will last very long.'

'What will you do then?'

'Ah!'

She produced triumphantly a somewhat bent cigarette from the bottom of her bag, where her hands had been blindly groping.

'Oh God, I hate myself,' she said, as she put it battered and all as it was into her mouth. 'No damn self-control. I mean to say, Joe Logan, where are you if you can't resist putting a small white tube full of poison into your mouth every half an hour?' She took some matches from her pocket and lit the cigarette. She took a deep pull on it. 'And what's more, it must be the most expensive poison in the world.'

He noticed she was wearing a ring with a small blue stone on her right hand.

'Are you engaged?'

She touched the ring for a moment with a finger and then pushed her hand into her pocket.

'Oh, that,' was all she said.

'I don't like my teacher.'

'I don't like quite a lot of my pupils.'

'Oh.'

'Perhaps it had never occurred to you that some of you, at times, are utterly unbearable.'

'You get paid for teaching us.'

'Not enough, Joe Logan, no way.'

'You could always do something else.'

'What would you suggest?'

'You could always get a job in a cigarette factory.'

She laughed and then threw her half-smoked cigarette over her shoulder into the middle of the road.

'Beastly boy. Now see what you've done, you've prolonged my life by ten minutes.'

'You'll thank me for that when the moment comes.'

'Maybe I will and maybe I won't. The Chinese . . . I think it's the Chinese . . . have a peculiar idea. If you save someone from death, you are responsible for the rest of their life . . . as if your own wasn't enough. So now you're responsible for ten minutes of my life.'

He considered the suggestion.

'I protest.'

'Too late.' She got up and pulled her coat around her. 'Come on. It's too cold to sit here any longer. Walk to the cigarette shop with me and I'll buy you a bar of chocolate.'

'No thanks.'

She didn't argue, just looked down at him with slight amusement.

'Tooraloo,' she said, and walked off down the hill swinging her briefcase.

'Mad.' He said the word quietly to himself as he looked after her.

Brendan was sitting at the kitchen table when he went in. His hair was long like a girl's and a soft moustache drooped around his mouth. Mam would hate all that. An anorak and a rucksack were on the floor beside him. He travelled light. The two of them stared at each other in silence.

'God, you've grown,' said Brendan eventually. 'You're not a babby any longer.'

'Hello.'

'I'd have passed you in the street, so I would.'

33

Joe couldn't think of anything to say.

'Mam won't like your hair.'

'That's not much of a welcome home. Are you glad to see me?'

Joe nodded

Brendan held his hand out across the table.

'Here, shake a fist. Feel me, I'm real.'

His hand was thin and engrained with travelling grime. Joe touched it briefly, almost nervously, and then sat down and looked at his brother, protected by the table from any sudden physical gesture.

'It's great you're back.'

'At last, a word of welcome. Where is everyone? How is everyone?'

'Mam's at work. Isn't he . . .?' He jerked his head towards the ceiling.

'There's not a soul about. His room is what you might call atmospheric.'

Joe smiled sourly.

'I suppose he's gone down the road.'

'Oh.'

'No one knew you were coming.'

'I said.'

'You didn't say today. Mam was going to write.'

'Oh.'

'Not to come. That was what she was going to say. Not to come.'

Brendan laughed slightly.

'She never changes.'

'No.'

'And he . . .?'

'He's never well.'

'But in himself?'

Joe drew a line along the oilcloth with his finger nail.

'He's a great old skin,' said Brendan at last.

'If you say so.'

'Maimed by life.'

Joe considered that remark.

'Maimed,' he said. 'That's good. He's that all right. Maimed.'

'You're only a kid. You wouldn't know what I'm talking about.'

'No?'

'Or what he is talking about.'

'Would you like a cup of tea?'

'Don't bother.'

'It's no bother. I always make one for him at this time, when he's in.'

'I had one on the train.'

'You came on the train?'

'Yeah.'

'That's nice. I'd like to go on a train.'

'It's O.K. I'd rather have my own . . . you know . . . vroom vroom.'

'Yes.'

They stared at each other across the table, studying with care each likeness, each difference.

'You've grown.'

'So you said. It'd be queer if I hadn't.'

'What teacher do you have?'

'Miss McCabe.'

'God, is she still going. I'm sorry for you.'

'There's worse. Mam won't like your hair.'

'If she doesn't like it she can lump it.'

'What was it like over there?'

'Great, man, really great.'

He took a small flat bottle from his pocket and put it on the table.

'Get us a glass, would you, there's a good chap?'

Joe got up and opened the cupboard. Brendan twisted and untwisted the cap on the bottle.

'There's none here,' said Joe. 'They must all be up in his room.'

'No matter.'

He took the top off the bottle and tilted it to his mouth. Joe watched the stretching of his throat as he swallowed. He put the bottle carefully on the table and screwed the top back on again. He wiped his mouth with the back of his wrist.

'Fantastic.' His hands began their fiddling again.

'Fantastic?'

'Yep. To begin with it's awful. You think, Jesus, why did I ever come to this dump, and then . . . suddenly it's O.K. Fantastic. It's all there. All happening. You could make a packet.'

'Why did you come back?'

Brendan took the cap right off the bottle again and looked at it in silence, or looked at something.

'I had to come,' he said eventually. Carefully he screwed the top on again and then moved the bottle across several squares on the oilcloth. The squares were red and white, scarred here and there by cigarette burns.

'Why? Had to?'

'You wouldn't understand.'

'I'm not thick.'

'You're too young.'

'Mam doesn't want you home.'

'I know.'

'She thinks, you know, you'll get mixed up with the Provies.'

'You were always her pet.'

'What's that got to do with it?'

Brendan shook his head.

'Are you?'

'Am I what?'

'Going to get mixed up . . .'

'Shut your damn face.'

He thumped his fist on the table and the bottle danced for a moment.

'Of course I'm not. I just couldn't stay there with this . . this . . . you wouldn't understand. Dad . . .'

36

'He won't understand. That's for sure. He doesn't understand anything. He'll just think you want to be a hero . . . like him.'

'You're a brat.'

'You'll never get a job here anyway, if that's what you're looking for.'

'I have shekels.'

His hand moved to his pocket and touched what might have been a bulging wallet.

'I worked hard over there. I have . . .'

'I remember the day you went away,' said Joe.

'Aye.'

Brendan rubbed his hand over his face in an unhappy gesture. Joe got up and went and stood beside him. He didn't like to touch him, but he stood as close to his brother as he possibly could.

'Are you not well?'

'I'm tired. It's odd being here. It's . . . Nothing in here has changed. You've grown. How dare you grow while I wasn't looking?'

They both laughed suddenly with relief.

'I think I'll have that cup of tea after all.'

'O.K.'

Joe went out to the scullery and filled the kettle. He wouldn't have known Brendan. He'd have passed him in the street too, he thought. His face after all those years was pale, city-coloured, like so many others who had gone away and come back. Like some of the ones from the prisons too. Their faces had the same look. It couldn't be all that fantastic if your face got like that. Shekels, that was a good word. He'd say that to someone. Someone like the girl on the wall. It was a word she might like. It sounded like gold and silver rather than dirty old pound notes. He carried the kettle into the kitchen and put it on the stove. The coal bucket was empty. He picked it up. His brother was sitting at the table staring at the dresser across the room as if it were a million miles away. Hills, rising gently into mountains. Mixing colours, moving light, shadows. Clouds that sometimes smothered the whole world. He had never been on top of a mountain and looked down at the world. That would really be something. He hadn't even been up on the city walls, not that he could remember anyway. Great curls of barbed wire and corrugated sheeting stopped you now. But Brendan would have other visions in his head. Out in the yard an evening drizzle had settled in. Greyness dropped from the grey sky, covering the walls and the sloping roofs. Mrs O'Toole's hens crooned softly in the next yard. There was a smell of smoke carried down with the rain. Somewhere something was burning. Back in the kitchen Brendan still stared into space. Joe rattled the cinders down to the bottom of the stove and then poured the coal in on top of the glowing embers. The kettle began to murmur.

'Do you want anything to eat, or will you wait till Mam gets back?'

'Huh?'

'You were asleep with your eyes open.'

'Yes. Sort of asleep. Dreaming anyway.'

'Some bread and jam? Something like that?'

'No thanks. Tea. Just tea. That'd be great.'

Joe put two cups and their saucers on the table.

'The same cups,' said Brendan, surprised, pleased also.

Joe put the tea into the pot and then poured in the boiling water. The leaves swirled to the top as he poured.

'They look like floating mouse droppings.'

'What do?' asked Brendan.

'The tea leaves.'

'Well, I hope they're not.'

'Do you take milk and sugar?'

'Of course I do. Don't you know that only Prods drink their tea without sugar.'

'Is that a fact?' Joe's voice was disbelieving.

'It's always been said, for what it's worth.'

'I wouldn't think it was worth much.'

38

'As snotty as ever.'

'I am not snotty.'

'You certainly used to be. Little yellow ribbons hanging all the time from your nose. I used to complain to Mam about it.'

Joe laughed.

'What did she say?'

'Wipe the little brat's nose yourself if you're so fussy.'

'I don't believe you.' The thought offended him slightly. He frowned. His hand trembled with a moment's anger as he poured out the tea and pushed the cup across the table towards his brother.

'Here.'

'Thanks, kiddo.' He yawned hugely, a yawn that showed Joe clearly all the complexities of the throat. 'God, I'm knackered. I could sleep a week.' He picked up his cup and blew ripples into it.

There was a fumbling at the door. They heard it open and then after a moment slam shut. There was a clink of bottles, a cough. Shuffling of feet as he pushed the bottles in behind the coats by the door.

'Have you my tea made?'

'Aye, I have.'

'That's a fella.' His voice was benign. He appeared in the doorway, panting slightly from his walk up the hill.

'A visitor.' One hand went up to smooth at his hair.

'Hardly,' said Brendan, standing up and taking a step towards his father.

'Ah now . . . look . . . Ah God, Brendan, welcome home . . . son.'

The man threw his hands out in front of him in an awkward gesture of welcome.

'Son.'

Brendan took another step towards his father. They both stared at each other like dogs at a street corner, and were silent.

'There's your tea.'

39

Joe banged another cup down on the table. Tea slopped over the top on to the oil cloth.

'Ah,' said his father.

He moved warily past Brendan, putting a hand out to touch his shoulder just at the last moment before lurching into his chair.

'You look . . . are you well? You've . . .'

He made a gesture with his hand that was a recognition of his son's adulthood.

'I mind so well the day you went.'

Joe saw quite clearly for a moment his brother's figure leaning as he went down the hill.

'Did you come home in an airplane?'

'Train and boat.'

'Aye.' Mr Logan's voice was disappointed. 'More sense, I suppose. Cheaper. Safer. You never can tell.'

He stirred his tea.

'Aye. Train and boat. Many's the time I did that crossing myself. Euston station, and the great greyness. I was young . . . and from Dublin too. I've done it from there. I wasn't a cripple then, I can tell you. No. The seagulls follow the boat. Do they?'

'I didn't notice.'

'All the way sometimes. It never took a feather out of me that journey. A whole crowd of us together. We'd earn a few bob and then come back. Rich. My whole days.' Tears trembled suddenly in his voice. 'If you get my meaning. Whole. Once I was whole. Then.'

Brendan pulled a chair up beside him and sat down.

'It's all right, Dad. I know.'

'Look at me now. If I'd known you were coming, son, I'd have stayed in. Something to look forward to. Something to make a day.'

'I told Mam.'

'Not the day. Not the time, you didn't.'

'I thought I'd surprise you all.'

'Tell you what, son. We'll hop down, you and I, and have

a quick one. See the boys. We'll be back before your mother gets home. Just one. What do you say?'

'Fine.'

'But . . .' said Joe.

'We'll be back,' said his father firmly, 'in plenty of time. Just to say hello to the boys. Just . . . Have you a couple of dollars?'

Brendan patted his pocket.

'Good lad. I had a bit of a bad day on the horses.'

'Mam . . .'

The old man pushed himself up with speed from the chair. His face had become almost lively.

'Ah give over, boy. Child.'

Brendan watched his father with a detached amusement, almost as if he had never met the man before.

'What'll I say to her? She'll be upset.'

'Don't go yammering on like that. There's no need for her to be upset. My son and I . . .' He took Brendan's arm and stood holding it for a moment to get his breath back. 'We . . . yes. We're just going to say hello to the boys. Hello. Just tell her that. There's no harm in that at all.'

'They said they were only going to say hello.'

He sat across the table from his mother, pushing the last of his chips around on his plate through the shiny egg yolk. He hated runny yolk. She would never take the time to make the eggs hard. She always made him eat up. The chips glistened with the yellow stickiness. He couldn't look at her face anymore, it was closed and angry. She had eaten nothing. She hadn't even put a plate for herself on the table, just smoked cigarette after cigarette, her fingers plucking them angrily from her mouth when they were too small to smoke any more and crushing them to death in a saucer.

'You said it,' she said. 'Fifteen times you said it. You shouldn't have let them go.'

'How could I stop them?'

'Eat up your chips.'

'I hate runny egg.'

'Eat your chips, I tell you. There's many have nothing to eat. Be thankful.'

'I met a nice girl today.'

As a conversation-changer it got him nowhere.

Joe sighed.

'She's a teacher.'

Silence. Indifference.

'She is smoking herself to death. So she says.'

'Death can't come, quick enough for me.'

'Ah, Mam.'

'Ah, Mam what?'

'You shouldn't say things like that.'

She stretched out a hand towards him. It was her tired left hand, even the weight of the thin gold ring seemed too much for it.

'Cherish your youth, son. It's the only good time.'

'It has its ups and downs,' he said, thinking of the equilateral triangle.

She smiled for the first time.

'Have you homework?'

'Mmmm.'

'Get on with it so and don't be sitting there wasting time.'

The two men came in as he was collecting up his books to go to bed. They seemed wrapped in a web of warmth and companionship, the smell of beer and cigarette smoke clinging around them, the tail end of spoken words and other men's laughter was still with them. His mother, who had sat, motionless, at the table while Joe worked, got to her feet as they came in the door.

'Hello, son.' Her voice was unwelcoming. Brendan edged slightly towards his father for some sort of protection.

'Great to see you, Mam. Great to be back. Fantastic . . .'

There was a long silence.

'Great.' He laughed. 'I've been away too long. Look at the size of the child, for God's sake.'

'Your tea is ruined.'

'That's all right, Mam. It'll be . . . great. I'm sorry.'

'Sorry nothing,' growled the father. 'Sorry, sorry, sorry, that's all she wants you to say. Sorry for this, sorry for that, sorry I was born. That's no way to greet your son, woman.'

She turned away from them and bent over the oven.

'Go to bed, Joe, there's a good lad. It's getting late.'

Joe finished packing his books into his schoolbag.

His father turned towards the stairs.

'I want no tea anyway.'

There was no reaction from his wife. She lifted a plate out of the oven and set it down on the top of the stove. She wiped carefully round the rim with the cloth in her hand.

He hauled himself on to the bottom step.

'Did you hear? No food. I have no appetite.'

She slammed the oven door shut with her knee.

'I'm away to my bed.' He coughed. 'I want nothing.'

'I'll give you a hand up the stairs, Dad.' Brendan moved towards him.

'Sit down.' Her voice was sharp. Brendan hesitated. 'Now. Sit down.' She put his plate on the table and pointed to a chair.

'He's well able to drag himself up the stairs.'

Brendan looked briefly at his father and then sat down. His egg was hard with a shining hard skin covering it like, Joe thought, as if you'd bought it just like that in a supermarket.

Brendan looked down at the food on his plate with an anger that was meant for his mother.

Joe held his schoolbag tightly under his arm and watched his father pull himself from step to step. There was nothing new in the operation, nothing even very pitiful.

'Nothing's changed,' he heard Brendan say. 'I mean here . . . In here. Not out beyond. You know, here.'

'I know well,' said his mother. 'Nothing ever changes. It only gets worse.'

Now that Brendan was home again Joe no longer had the luxury of a room to himself. His clothes had been pushed up to one end of the press, the table by his bed was gone and the camp bed that had lain for years under his own bed had been put up across the middle of the floor. There was no floor space left, only a thin strip of worn linoleum between the two beds. His precious bowl of stones that he had kept on the table, carefully covered with water so that they would keep the shine of their colours, had been shoved on top of the cupboard. One of his blankets had been removed and was doubled neatly over on top of the camp bed . . . He knew, with resignation, that it would only be a matter of time before he was asked to give up his bed to Brendan. It was still dark when he woke in the morning and the room was filled with a strange smell, half sweat, half alcohol, which almost choked him. He could hear Mam moving downstairs. He got up and pulled his clothes off the end of the bed. Brendan grunted once or twice, but slept on. He definitely wouldn't be long on that camp bed, thought Joe sourly, as he looked at the dark mound of his body, with one hand trailing on the floor. Joe tiptoed out of the room, clutching his clothes, and went down the stairs to wash in the scullery. His mother was shaking corn flakes into his bowl. The lid of the kettle rattled. It was warm, only the floor under his bare feet was cold and still wet from the scrubbing she must have given it not long before. She was wearing a brown overall on top of her work clothes and her red slippers, with white nylon fur that fluffed out over her ankles, that she had bought herself the Christmas before. She had wrapped them in Christmas paper and put them on the table beside his present, a handkerchief with her initial embroidered on it in blue thread, and the mystery parcel from Brendan. She had opened his parcel first, he remembered, and thanked him with a dry kiss on his cheek and then gingerly touched the parcel from England as if it might explode if handled roughly. It contained a tiny bottle of

44

scent. Carefully she had unscrewed the gold lid and then pulled out a little rubber plug with the tips of her nails. She poured a dot of the liquid on to the first finger of her left hand and rubbed it behind one ear and then the other. The sweet smell reached him across the table. She pushed the stopper back into the bottle and then put the lid on. She put the tiny bottle back into its box. There were silver stars on the outside of the box and Joe hoped that she might give it to him one day to keep things in, but he didn't think that she had ever used the scent again, just kept the unopened box on the dressing table in her room. The smell had made her seem for a few moments like a different person. After all that she had opened her own parcel.

'Just what I wanted,' she said, as she put them side by side on the table for him to admire.

Her voice was ironical, she was herself again.

'Who gave you those yokes anyway?' asked his father, who never gave anyone presents, even at Christmas.

'The only person who loves me.'

'Poor eejit' was his only comment.

The slippers had remained on the table throughout the meal. No one had ever mentioned them again.

'No sign of Brendan waking?' she asked as he came in from the scullery and sat down.

He shook his head.

She picked a saucepan off the stove and poured hot milk over his corn flakes. He hated hot milk on his corn flakes, they all went soggy and tasted of warm cardboard, but there was never any use arguing with her. Then he always had two pieces of toast with either runny butter or jam. Money doesn't grow on trees. And a cup of tea, or two if he had the time. She drank her own tea as she moved around settling the place, wiping the top of the stove, mopping out the scullery, washing and wringing out the tea towels and hanging them up above the stove to dry.

'He'll have to get his own breakfast so. I can't be hanging on here for him. He can't expect me to be running round after him. He's not a child. He doesn't need caring for any longer. He'll have to get that into his head of he's going to stay here.'

'I don't need caring for,' said Joe, through a mouthful of toast.

'That's a matter of opinion.'

'I help, don't I? Do things. The fire and things.'

'You do, son. My teeth are paining me.'

'They're always paining you. You should go to the dentist. At school they're always going on about us going to the dentist.'

'And what good would that do me? He'd only take them out. God knows I'm no film star, but I'd rather be with my teeth than without them.'

There was a long pause.

'Your Dad has all his teeth yet. Not a bit of trouble with them in all these years. He had lovely teeth in his day. He's an old man.' She repeated the words fiercely. 'An old man.'

'Why did he come back?'

'Who? Your socks are there on the stove. Do you want an apple? I'll get you one to put in your bag.'

'No thanks.'

'Ah, take an apple. It'll be a bit of good inside you.'

She took an apple from a paper bag in the cupboard and put it on the table beside him.

'Fruit does you good.'

He might be able to swap it for something better.

'But why, Mam? He had a good job over there. He was making a packet.'

'You shouldn't believe everything you hear.'

'You mean you think he's lying?'

'I'm not committing myself. He should be a good boy. That's all I have to say.'

She went out into the passage and he could hear her sweeping the dust along the lino, banging the brush against the wall as she moved towards the door.

46

My brother has come home.

Why?

That's what I would like to know.

That's what I ask myself from time to time.

He has money rattling in his pockets.

Money that folds in his wallet.

He says he earned it by working very hard.

Over there he worked.

Making a packet.

How?

My mother says I shouldn't believe everything I'm told.

Why not?

He chewed the plastic end of his pen. It was all much easier if you didn't have to make rhymes. But, then, was it poetry at all. There were people wrote it like that, he knew that for sure. He had read it. It was rhythms that mattered, so that it didn't sound like ordinary sentences.

A hand was clamped on to his shoulder. There was a murmur of laughter.

'How many times have I told you, Joseph, that the classroom is for working in? Don't bother to answer me, I doubt if you can count that far.'

She removed her hand. The laughter swelled hopefully.

'It'll have to be the head this time.'

'Sorry, miss.'

'Sorry.' She spoke the word with contempt.

His hand crept over the paper, covering the so-called poem.

'Do sums bore you so much?'

'Yes, miss.'

Someone laughed aloud.

Her face became dark with anger.

'No laughing. This is no laughing matter.' She banged her clenched fist on the desk beside Joe's book.

'How do you pass your time? I feel I have a right to know. It is also my time.'

She plucked the paper out from under his fingers. His

writing danced sideways away from him as she pulled. His face boiled as she held the paper up and read what he had written silently. After a moment she laid the paper down in front of him again.

'In the long run, Joseph, sums would stand you in better stead.'

'Yes, miss.'

'Ten years ago I would have given you a good walloping, but progress . . .' She moved away from him towards the front of the class.

'I don't want to waste the head's time as well as yours and mine. I'll give you extra homework. I am angry.'

'I'm sorry . . .'

'As I said before I don't want your sorrow. I want your attention. Do you call that poetry?'

Someone laughed. She raised her head and stared down the length of the room at whoever it was.

'Well . . .' he hesitated.

'A waste of time.'

She picked up the chalk and drew a circle on the board. One of last year's bluebottles buzzed hopelessly in a corner of the window. The sun came out from behind a cloud and for a moment the room was filled with dancing dust. She drew a line across the centre of the circle.

'The diameter,' she said. 'Are you all paying attention?'

'Yes, miss.'

The diversion was over.

'This is becoming a habit. Almost a habit.'

'Hello, Kathleen.' He said her name with diffidence.

'Not kept in today?'

He grinned.

'No. I have extra homework though.'

'You must be the bane of your teacher's life.'

'She's the bane of my life. What does it mean anyway?'

'A sort of walking talking nightmare. What were you up to this time?'

'I wasn't listening. I was wasting her time and my time, the whole world's time.'

'Why don't you go and play with your friends when you come out?'

'Mam doesn't like me to. It's because of . . . well . . . you know, the way things are.'

'You might be lured to the barricades.'

'Something like that.'

'Or be killed by a stray bullet from the soldiers and become a hero. A national hero.'

'Like my father. Mam wouldn't want two heroes in the family.'

'Is your father a hero?'

'He says he is anyway.'

They both laughed.

'Tell you what,' she said. 'I only live up the hill a little bit. Come on home and have a cup of tea with me. It's too cold to stand around here. Or would your mother mind?'

'I wouldn't have to tell her, would I?'

'You can suit yourself.'

'Thanks then, that would be nice.'

They walked in silence up the road, leaning slightly forward against the wind. She fished in her pocket for the cigarettes and put one in her mouth. She didn't light it though, just rolled it from side to side as she walked. They came to a terrace of high grey houses with steps rising steeply up to the doors from the pavement. At the first one she stopped and lit the cigarette.

'Here we are.' Smoke trickled from her nose as she spoke. 'I told you it wasn't far.'

He followed her up the steps. In the long dark hall there was a faint smell of gas and damp clothes, which faded as they went up the stairs. Her room was on the first floor with a window that looked across the road and through the empty windows of a burnt-out house. The windows stared back at him as he tried to make sense of the glimpses of light and

shadow that he could see beyond them. They were unfriendly.

'Do you like Jaffa cakes?'

He turned away from the window.

'Yes.'

'It's just as well. They're all I've got.'

'This is where you live?'

She laughed.

'Yes.'

'Why are you laughing?'

'It's such an odd question to ask. It really is.'

'Have you no family? A mother or father or something
like that?'

'Nope.'

'Oh.'

'Mothers or fathers have I none.'

The gas lit with a pop and blue flames spread up the face
of the fire and then slowly turned to orange. He moved
towards the warmth.

'Brothers or sisters?'

'No.'

The conversation wasn't exactly swinging.

'You're alone so?'

'Do you want tea or cocoa?'

He considered the question.

'How do you make your cocoa?'

'A good point. Lots of milk, no water and as much sugar
as you want.'

'O.K.,' he said. 'That'll do fine.'

'Sit down. Take the weight off your feet.'

She took her coat off and hung it on the back of the door.
He sat down on the divan and looked around. There was a
table covered with books and papers, an armchair, two
upright chairs, a sink and a small cooker in the corner,
above which were some shelves that held plates and cups
and some more books. A large cupboard was half-open and
bursting with clothes and suitcases and frying pans and

what looked to Joe like a box overflowing with pairs of shoes. There was a heap of coloured cushions on the divan, which was covered with a brightly striped rug. There was another pop from the gas in the cooker.

'I'll have some cocoa too,' she said, emptying a bottle of milk into a saucepan.

'Why do you have a carpet on your bed?'

'Why not? You don't have to put carpets on the floor, you know. You can hang them on the walls, put them on the bed, even cut them up and make clothes of them if you want to. It's the same with most things really. You mustn't be too rigid about things. Look at every object with an open mind.'

'You could be a little mad.'

'I could,' she agreed, smiling. 'But where's the harm? The great thing is to make the most out of what you've got. What did I do with my poison?'

'There, beside the cooker.'

'Ah, yes.'

She took a deep drag and put the cigarette down in the saucer again.

'Some people believe they have nothing. Then life gets very bad.' She put two cups down side by side on the table, lining them up evenly, handles symmetrically sideways, as if it mattered.

'You have nice things.'

'Mmmm.'

'These mugs. They're nice.'

'I got them in London. There's a lot of things for buying in London, millions of people all buying, buying.'

'My brother's just come back. Did I tell you about him?'

'Oops.'

The milk rushed up the side of the saucepan and over the top on to the stove before she had time to stop it.

'Blast.'

She grabbed a cloth and mopped at the milk.

'It always does that. Even if I'm staring at it, glaring at it, willing it to behave, it does it just the same.'

51

She poured the milk into two mugs and stirred in the cocoa.

'Here. Take care, it's blazing.'

She threw the cloth into the sink and came and sat down beside him on the divan, cigarette and mug clutched in the same hand.

'Sorry for all that . . . you were saying something about your brother?'

'Brendan.'

'That's a nice name. I like it better than Joe.'

He blew into his cocoa and watched the rings expand out to the sides of the mug. Skin might form, he thought with distaste.

'Is it good?'

'What?'

'Brendan being home? He's been away a long time, hasn't he?'

'Yes. Ages. A couples of years. I was only a kid.'

She smiled. He felt himself blush.

'Are you pleased he's back?'

'I don't honestly know. I've hardly seen him. It'll take . . . like a while . . . you know . . .'

He paused.

'. . . to . . . to . . .'

'Come to terms.'

She leant forward and stubbed out the cigarette butt in the grate. Smoke squirmed out from under her fingers and then died. He wondered for a moment if she was a Protestant.

'Used you to like him?'

'I don't remember. That's all I remember, then he went away.'

She got up and wandered aimlessly round the room, picking things up and putting them down again. He supposed she was looking for her cigarettes.

'Mam is upset.' He threw the words after her wandering figure.

'She's afraid he'll get into trouble. Mixed up . . . you

52

know . . . She worries a lot about that sort of thing. Like me being home from school quickly. I told you . . .'

'Yes,' she said.

She found them in the pocket of her coat, and sighed with relief. She came back and sat down again.

'She has all the worrying to do.'

'Some people quite like that, you know, Joe. They need to be worrying away all the time.'

He looked down at his cocoa, which was forming a crinkled skin across the top. 'I don't think she likes it. You know the way some people have happy faces?'

'Yes.'

'Well, she hasn't. Not even when she's watching TV. I watch her a lot. I've skin on my cocoa.'

'It won't kill you.'

'I don't like it. It makes me feel sick.'

'There's a spoon over there.' She nodded towards the sink. 'Scoop it off.'

He got up and carried his mug across the room. Outside, the almost dark sky was streaked with gold. There was a red plastic spoon on the draining board. He performed the delicate operation, dropping the skin quickly into the basin. It reminded him of a burst balloon, something else that he hated.

'She works four days a week in the Strand Café.'

'What does she do there?'

He thought for a moment.

'She performs menial tasks.'

He sat down again and sipped tentatively at his drink, hoping against hope that he hadn't left any shreds of skin behind that might touch his lips.

'That can't be very nice for her.'

'It's not. But someone has to keep the home together.' He smiled at her. 'That's what she says.'

'And your father? What does he do?'

'He's not well at all.'

'Oh.'

She put her mug on the floor and started on the cigarette-lighting business.

'My mother says he's a retired hero.' He looked at her. Her face was a serious, listening face.

'That's a sort of joke really.'

The light from the match patterned her face for a moment with orange and black. 'Wounded in the Civil War. He has a bad leg . . . and his back . . . well . . . He ought to have a pension. He says the Free State government is shirking its legitimate responsibilities. He says . . . he says . . . anyway he's not at all well.'

'He must be getting on if he fought in the Civil War,' was all she said.

'Yes. He's old all right. He says . . . well, he says a lot of things, but Mammy says you shouldn't believe everything you hear. She says that a lot.'

'I can see your mother's point of view. For myself, I prefer to believe most things cautiously.'

'Are you a Protestant?'

She threw her head back and roared with laughter.

'What gives you that idea?'

He blushed.

'I hope you don't mind. I just . . . I don't know really.'

'I don't mind a bit. My mother was. So how clever you are. A positive mind-bending mind-reader.'

'I'd like to be handy with words. Like you. You are.'

'I'm sure you will be one day.'

'The cocoa's good.'

'In spite of the skin?'

He nodded.

'Have another biscuit?'

'Yes. Thanks.'

Two men ran along the street and round the corner, the metal on their heels sparking the pavement as they ran. She gave a little shiver and got up. She went over to the window and peered out and then, even though it wasn't yet dark, she pulled the curtains tight together. Keeping safety in. The

54

safe room glowed in the warmth from the gas fire. The curtains were of some heavy brown material and her hand looked very white against them. It looked almost like a bird from where he sat watching.

'Soon the spring will come,' she said, her hand still holding together the edges of the curtains. 'Nothing ever seems so bad in the spring.'

'And then the summer,' he said.

She came over and sat down beside him again.

'I'll be gone then.'

'Oh.'

'My job was only for the year. I'll have to go then. I must say . . .'

She leant forward and blew the surface of her cocoa, blew the wrinkled skin over to one side and then took a sip.

'I didn't know you were going.'

'I have to.' She smiled to herself. 'I have a commitment elsewhere.'

'Don't you like it here?'

'I like it all right. It's not that.'

'Are you feared?'

She considered before speaking.

'I suppose so. I'm afraid of something awful happening. I don't just mean bombs and all that. You get sort of used to that in a horrible way, but something deeply awful . . . I can't explain. Words are aggravating the way they hide on you when you need them most. We must do a lot of things together, you and I, before I go. If you'd like to, that is . . .'

'That'd be O.K.'

'Good.'

She put out a hand and touched his knee.

'Drink up, there's a good boy. I wouldn't want your mother to be worried. I'll walk part of the way home with you.'

'You needn't bother.'

He felt, suddenly, that he was being treated as a child.

'No bother. I have to get my evening's supply of poison.'

He sipped slowly at his drink, not wanting to be rushed or pushed around.

'I can never correct the books without puffing away. Otherwise I give everyone terrible marks.' She laughed. 'Isn't that stupid?'

'I always get terrible marks anyway.'

'Only because you don't care. You're the sort of pupil drives teachers mad. Full of ability, but not caring a halfpenny.'

For some reason she switched on the radio which was on the floor beside her. It was a fidget really, he decided, rather than a desire to hear anything. 'Now we have time to kill,' sang some young men, their voices clear, syncopated.

'Kill the shadows on our skin,

Kill the fire that burns within,

Killing time, my friend.'

Dreamtime. The words danced into Joe's mind.

'Killing time, my friend.'

Under the words the music jigged. Dreamtime. The mug drooped in his fingers.

'Mind,' she said. 'Oh, mind.'

A stream of cocoa poured on to the floor. He righted the mug with a jerk of his wrist.

'I'm sorry. I'll . . .'

'No. Don't bother. I'll do it.'

She fetched a cloth from the sink and stooped over.

'Now we have time to kill . . .' Quicker than before.

'Kill the shadows on our skin. Kill the . . .'

'Poor old time.'

She looked up at him, her face red from stooping.

'People are always killing time. Some people do nothing else all their lives . . . killing time before it kills them.' She laughed briefly. 'I think someone else must have said that before me.'

'I see the last black swan

Fly past the sun.

I wish I, too, were gone
Back home again.'
He drained the remains of his cocoa down his throat, skin
and all, forcing the soft pieces down with difficulty, penance
for his carelessness.

'It seems our fortunes lied . . .'

'We'd better go,' she said, rinsing the cloth under the tap.

'Despite our gain.'

'First good Saturday. Sun, you know. We'll go up in the
hills. Grianan or somewhere. Would you like that?'

'I wouldn't mind.'

'Our tears fall like our pride. We cry in shame.'

'Not a very enthusiastic response.' She handed him his
anorak.

'I'd like it a lot, but you probably have other things to do.'

'Now we've got time to kill . . .'

'I probably haven't. Have you ever been to Grianan?'

He shook his head.

'Well that's a date them. We'll bring hard-boiled eggs.
I love hard-boiled eggs.'

'Kill the fire that burns within . . .'

She opened the door and they went out on to the landing.

'Aren't you going to turn the radio off?'

She closed the door on the voices.

'Killing time, my . . .'

'I hate going into dark lonely rooms.'

He understood.

The unfriendly smell still clutched at him as he tapped
across the lino. Outside there was shouting coming from
across the hill. No one was about. Even the shop on the
corner was empty. The owner was putting up the shutters
as they arrived.

'How's yourself?' he asked Kathleen and nodded to Joe.

'You're closing early.' She handed him the money for the
cigarettes.

'You're damn right I am. It's the first dry night we've had

for weeks and I'm not taking any chances. If anyone wants to break the place up they can do it when I'm not there. I've had the lads in twice demanding money, they can get it from someone else tonight. Twenty Carrolls. We have the granny staying and I'm taking the wife out for a drink across the border. A break. A bloody break.'

'Everyone needs a break,' agreed Kathleen.

'I hear your brother's home, Joe?'

'Aye . . . He's home.'

'More fool he.'

There was a wave of shouting from down the hill, and the sound of glass breaking.

'I believe he was making good money over there.'

'I wouldn't know,' said Joe, with caution.

'More fool he.' He picked the money up from the counter and looked at it for a moment and then put it into his pocket.

'I'll tell you something,' he said. 'They'll not get my cash the night and that's for sure. If I have to spend it all. I voted for McAteer all the years. Regular I voted and I'll vote for John Hume so I will, but I'm damned if I'll go on letting those gawbeens in here taking the money out of my till. It gets me, that's what it does. Four times I've had to put new glass in them windows. And I'll tell you another thing, Nationalist or no Nationalist, if this lot goes on, the minute my wains is out of school it's over to England on the first boat they'll go. My God, tonight. Here.'

He took a bar of Cadburys milk chocolate down from the shelf and held it out to Joe.

'Oh, no thanks, I couldn't.'

'Go on, take it. You might as well, better you than some others I could mention.'

Joe took the chocolate from his hand.

'Thanks,' he muttered.

'Goodnight,' said Kathleen, pushing Joe out into the street. 'Have a good evening.'

'I will if it's the last thing I do.' He slammed the door

behind them and they could hear him clattering the bolts home.

Kathleen and Joe began to laugh.

'I bet he'll get pissed,' said Joe, unwrapping his chocolate. 'Have a bit?'

'Out of his mind and he'll regret the whole thing tomorrow.'

'I bet the Provos will be waiting for him when he gets here in the morning. Your money or your life.'

'No money. He'll let them have the edge of his tongue, what's left of it.'

'And all the bars of Cadburys chocolate.'

'Yes please, I'd love a bit.'

She took a piece from his outstretched hand and put it into her mouth.

'I don't know why we were laughing. It's not really funny.'

'I'll go this way now.'

They stopped at the corner of the street leading down the hill. The houses leaned together for support, grey against red, red against mauve, mauve against a tired white. each roof slightly higher than the one next to it. The curve of the road was gentle, the windows were now full of light.

'Do you live down there?'

He nodded.

'Which house?'

He pointed vaguely, suddenly feeling, to his own surprise, the desire to keep a spark of privacy.

'Mmm,' she said. She patted his shoulder with an awkward gesture. 'See you, kid.' She gave a little laugh and turned and walked away, back the way they had come. He stood at the corner and watched her stooping a little over a lighted match. She paused for a moment and her face was once more illuminated by the tiny flicker of flame.

Later that night the army came and lifted Sean Buckley.

Joe didn't know, at the time, whose house they were at,

59

whose voices were shouting, whose door was being battered down. He lay stiff on the camp bed listening as the boots thudded down the street past their own house, and the battering started on a door across the road.

'All out, all out. Every fucking one of you out.' The door went in with a crash. A child began to cry.

He knew by Brendan's stillness that he also was awake and listening.

'What's up?' Brendan's voice was a whisper.

'They're lifting someone.'

Glass broke and scattered on the road.

'Who is it?' Brendan sat up and pulled at the curtains.

'I haven't the foggiest. You're best not to go near the window. In case there's shooting.'

Brendan lay down again. The springs creaked with the movement of his body.

'Over there against the wall.'

There was a mutter of voices. The child continued to cry.

'Kids and all. Madam.'

There was laughter from some man at the use of the word. A sound of splintering wood.

'Who is it?'

'I don't know, I tell you. Buckleys or maybe Foys.'

'Bastards.'

'Sssh.'

'Sssh? Why sssh? They can't hear. Why ssssh? Bastards.'

'You never can tell.'

'Fool.'

Suddenly there was a single shot. With a crack it hit a wall somewhere and then whined off down the street. Joe ducked back into his pillow. Fool. For a moment the child stopped crying and then began to bawl. The soldiers ran for cover. Their boots must have been sending up sparks in all directions, Joe thought. He'd seen that happen before.

A woman's voice shouted.

'For God's sake let the wains back in the house.'

60

'Mrs Buckley,' said Joe.

'Not fucking likely, missus. Anything comes our way comes their way too. Get back against that wall.'

'Have you got the boy?' A voice of authority. A voice like you hear on the TV. A voice that told people what to do.

'We've got a boy, sir.'

'Right. Get out of here quick before there's any more shooting. Next time someone might get hit. Come on, corporal, get them all out quickly.'

There was a rush of boots up the street, and then the sound of armoured cars being driven away. It was all over very quickly. Suddenly the only sound in the street was the child crying. The noise of the engines whined away and then the street filled with people. Someone started sweeping the glass with long even sweeps, a background to the rising hubbub of voices and the hysterical wailing of Mrs Buckley.

'Yes,' said Joe. 'It's Mrs Buckley all right.'

Brendan knelt up on his bed and peered out through the curtains. Joe just lay on the camp bed and stared at the ceiling. Through the wall he could hear his father giving out. His voice was full of drink and rose and fell in indignant cadences. He cried out about injustice and freedom and castigated himself for being the possessor of a body too weak to be able to strike the blows that had to be struck. He cried. There was a banging on the wall.

'Will you shut up,' shouted Mam's voice. 'For God's sake, and let us sleep.' Her voice was angry.

Brendan got down from the bed and went out of the room. Joe heard him open the door of his father's room and go in. He heard the creaking floorboards and the rattle of the bedsprings. His father's voice quietened. The two men's voices twisted together, patterned in his mind with the voices in the street, turned after a while into the jigging tune he had heard on the radio. Killing time my friend now we have time to kill kill the shadows killing time kill the fire

61

kill the fire killing time kill the swan the shadows on our . . . then soon, remarkably soon, there was nothing.

In the morning when he woke it was as if nothing had happened. Brendan's smell blanketed the small room. Downstairs his mother was grey and cross and only spoke to tell him to hurry up or he'd be late for school.

'What happened at the Buckleys after?'

'Get on with your breakfast.'

He knew it was no use discussing anything with her.

He got home from school on time that afternoon. He had loitered the whole way along the streets, pausing at corners, resting his arm from the weight of his school bag, staring into windows, counting the speckled patches of blue in the sky, but she never appeared. The wind had got up to almost storm force and the cardboard and plywood fillings in the broken windows banged and rattled, sounding like demons in behind the walls trying to batter their way out into the sleet-chilled air. He felt let down. Perhaps she had gone home another way, just to avoid seeing him. Perhaps he had bored her to death yesterday. He had a quick vision of her lying interestingly dead among the cushions on the divan. The doctor putting his instruments into his bag. Boredom killed her. A massive overdose of boredom. Poor girl. Poor nice girl. Laughter choked out of him and a woman passing with a shopping bag looked curiously at him. It's well for some to find anything to laugh at, her face seemed to say.

Two men were hammering plywood into place covering the Buckleys' empty windows. A very small child laboured up the hill on a very small tricycle, pushing the ground away from under him with his feet.

They were talking to each other in low voices across the table when he went into the kitchen, leaning towards each other, like plotters, as if they needed to drop their words quietly, directly into each other's ear. Brendan straightened up when his brother came into the room and nodded. Mr Logan continued to talk. The air was heavy with cigarette smoke, the table and the floor around it were littered with papers. Dirty dishes were stacked by the sink.

'If they'd ask me . . . that's all I need . . . ask me. I have it all at my finger tips.' Joe went over and looked into the stove. Down at the bottom of the darkness was a small red glimmer. He picked up the hod.

'I'll do that, Joe,' said Brendan.

'You didn't though. It'll go out.'

'I'll do it.'

Joe put the hod on the floor again.

'Not only have I the experience but I've read the books. Lots of the books. Haven't I had all the time in the world to read the books. I've read them so I have.'

He massaged the back of his neck with his hand for a moment.

'I mean to say . . .'

'Will you do it before Mam comes in?'

'I said I'll do it, I'll do it.'

'. . . these young lads haven't the experience. How can they have? They need the old fellas so they do. It stands to reason. Like last night. What were they at last night? Where was their marksman? If they'd had any gumption at all they'd have knocked off one of those soldiers. Sit down, can't you.'

Joe was edging towards the door.

'I have homework to do.'

'Here.'

Brendan pushed the papers off the table. Mr Logan took aim with an imaginary hand gun. Held out at arm's length in front of him it was, his left hand carefully supporting the arm. His head was ducked slightly to one side, his eyes narrowed, judging.

'There was few could better me.' His finger tightened on the trigger. 'Few. Could. Better. Me.' As he spoke each word he fired, the gun moving slowly from one corner of the room to the next. He put the gun down finally on the table and looked with satisfaction at his eldest son.

'I had a good eye. It's a great thing to have that so it is.'

'Yes,' said Brendan, obviously somewhat taken aback by the exhibition. Joe wondered who his father had killed with his four shots. Who, from his past, had been lined up on the other side of the tiny room? Had his hand shaken then as it shook now? Hard for a marksman to have a shaking hand, no matter how good his eye.

'Up there in the roof gullies. Head well down so they couldn't spot you. Couldn't get you. Pick one off and then away over the roof ridges and down the other side. Down through the skylight of a safe house. God.'

He rubbed his hand over his face.

'God be with the days.'

'I thought you were in a flying column,' said Joe.

His father crashed his fist down on the table.

'Wherever they needed me, son. Versatile you might have called me. First of the guerillas we were. Aye. First we were.'

Brendan yawned and stretched his arms above his head. His nails were bitten well below the tops of his fingers and the exposed flesh was puckered and sore-looking.

'I need air.'

'A dander down the road?'

'Mmm.'

'A quiet saunter. Filling the lungs. I'll be with you. The atmosphere in here is poisoned so it is. Give me a pull up out of this, son. Agility has left me. Uh unh.'

He grunted with effort and possible pain as Brendan helped him to his feet. He stood poised for a moment before he took his first step forward, his hands tightly clenched at his sides, as if he were waiting to lash out at some invisible opponent. Invincible man in his own mind. How big a sin is it to hate? wondered Joe. Or does the black emotion not matter as long as it is contained inside you?

'I know what you're thinking,' said his father, stepping with care towards the door. 'Believe you me, I know. Have you a few bob, Brendan?'

Brendan nodded.

'I have.'

'Let's get out so.'

He made the doorway and leant his weight against it for a moment, then straightened up to meet the outside world. Brendan turned to Joe, making a tiny gesture with his hands. It could have been apology.

'Tell Mam we'll be back in time for tea. We won't be long. Just a breath of air . . . a jar . . . the sitting in all day gets you down.' He smiled. It was a sweet smile that lit his pale face as if he had moved into a sudden beam of light. 'Honestly.'

Joe nodded.

Brendan lowered his voice to a whisper.

'He likes the company . . . needs it . . . you must see.'

Joe nodded again. There didn't seem to be much point in discussing anything.

'Tooraloo,' said Brendan.

'See you,' said Joe.

'Come on out of that before your mother comes in,' shouted their father from the hall.

Joe listened until he could no longer hear the sound of their feet and the mutter of their voices going up the hill, then angrily he began to rattle out the stove. He carried the ashes out into the back yard and tipped them into the dustbin. A bright cold moon grinned in the polished evening blue of the sky. The smell of the gas works blew on the air, Ash puffed up from the bin, choking his nose. He stood still with the ash pan in his hand listening to the sounds of people living that somehow you never seemed aware of in the day-time. A baby crying, the clatter of cups, the rise and fall of television voices, laughter, the creak of a door, each sound quite clear and individual, and of course, but now far away, the inevitable ambulance. The walls between the houses would be silver soon under the moon and frost would sparkle on the roofs.

'Now we've got time to kill,' he sang, and laughed at the

raucousness of his own voice. He'd never make it to the top twenty.

'Cherook,' said a hen in the next yard.

He felt cold.

'Cherook,' he said, just to be friendly, and went back into the house.

'Five were lifted last night.' As Brendan spoke he worked at a piece of bread on his plate with a finger until it turned into a grey, inedible lump.

They were sitting as the perfect family should sit in apparent peace around the table. The mother poured golden tea from a large tin pot.

'They ask for it,' she said, lifting a flowered cup and passing it to the father across the table. He grunted.

Anyone coming in now, Joe thought to himself, would think how nice. How lovely. That's what they'd think.

'Come on now, Mam, you know as well as I do there's some inside have never lifted a finger, said a word . . .'

'They're few and far between. If you go round creating destruction you ask for what you get. They're too kind to some of them.'

'Are you against the whole movement? Is that what it is?'

She picked up the teapot again and pulled another cup towards her. 'I want to live a decent life.'

'Isn't that what they want too? For you? hey? Isn't that it?'

'I'm not tangling with you, Brendan. I'm tired. I'm not the only tired person in this city.'

He leaned across the table and drummed with a fist. The teacups in their saucers rattled.

'There'll be no decent life for anyone here until we get the British out.'

'We?'

She smiled at him and handed him a steaming cup.

'Will you stop thumping on the table like that, you're spilling everything.'

66

'Every man jack of us.'

'There's many don't think the way you do.'

'Then they're traitors. To Ireland and to their class and . . .' he leaned even closer to her '. . . to their religion.'

He sat back in his chair again.

'I'm with you, son. I'm with you.' The old man's voice was soft with drink and illness.

'Don't you bring religion into your ravings. The brave carry-on of the lot of you must make Christ weep. Weep.' She shouted the word at her son and then, exhausted by her outburst, she clutched her arms around herself as if she were trying to hold her bones from falling apart.

'I'm with you, son.'

She looked at the old man with contempt, but made no remark.

There was a long silence.

'What good does killing do?' she asked eventually.

'Sometimes killing is necessary.'

'And what about the dead? Do they feel that?'

'Ah Mam, be your age. You know what I'm talking about. You never used to be a fool.'

'Run up to your room, Joe, and do your homework.'

'I've none to do.'

'Don't give me that.'

'It's true, Mam. Honest it is.' He crossed his fingers tightly under the table.

'You never used to talk like you do now, Mam.'

'Quit it, Brendan. Does it not enter your head that there's a rare difference between sitting round and listening to a bunch of old men telling their hero stories and what is happening now. I've learned a bit of sense. I see only sadness. So much for the heroes.'

'If Ireland was free . . .'

'Words.'

'The Tans in their big Crossley tender . . .' sang the father in his tired voice.

'Words. Words. Words. God. If I'd've had the guts I'd've

67

left you. To drown in your words. I've no doubt that in forty years' time, or in fifty maybe, you'll be doing the same thing as he is now. All I can say is I'm glad I won't be round to see you.'

'She's a hard woman all right,' said the old man. 'I always told you that. A hard one. It's the only word for her. Hard.' A sob of self-pity came out of him as he repeated the word. She got up and began to clear the dishes from the table. She piled the plates and cups on the draining board and poured hot water from the kettle into the sink. The old man and the young one looked at her inimically as she moved backwards and forwards between the scullery and the table. As she turned on the cold tap the water rattled in the pipes.

'I think I'll go to bed.' Joe stood up.

'Are your shoes clean for school?'

'Clean enough.'

Normally she would have looked, but this evening she didn't turn from the sink. This upset him. He pushed past her into the scullery and took the shoe cloth out of the box where the polish was kept and gave his shoes a quick rub. It didn't make much difference, if any, to their appearance, but it made him feel better.

'Obscure!'

The word came into his mind and he said it out aloud.

'Obscure. Ob . . . scure . . . lure . . . pure . . . hoor.' He laughed to himself. 'A pure hoor dressed in velours is pretty obscure.'

His mother had turned round from the sink and was looking at him.

'What's up with you?'

He put the cloth back in the box.

'I was just talking to myself. That's all.'

'I hope you find yourself entertaining.'

'Always,' he answered. That was the truth anyway.

He opened the back door and looked out into the yard. The wind was cold. He wondered what she would be doing

68

now. Would she be asleep, he wondered, or be lying curled on the divan listening to the radio? Correcting books, puffing as she frowned over the inadequacies of her pupils, or just asleep, obscurely asleep, the light from the wind-shaken lamp outside in the street making patterns on the floor?

'Will you for heaven's sake shut that door, or you'll have us all blown out of the house.'

He pushed the door shut against the wind and decided not to wash. He'd cleaned his shoes at any rate.

'Good night.' He pushed past her and walked slowly through the kitchen. The two men were sitting staring into space, the space behind their skulls. Brendan's fingers drummed unconsciously and nervously on the table. Behind him his mother pulled the scullery door shut and locked it.

'Life is very obscure,' he said at the bottom of the stairs. No one seemed interested.

It was a quiet night. It was always hard to know why some nights there seemed to be no problems. Even the wind creeping round the corners was relaxed, while other nights, even if there was no trouble, were full of fear and waiting shadows.

As Joe woke in the morning Brendan turned over in the big bed and coughed. Then Joe saw the darkness of his arm stretch up against the grey window. Below, Mam rattled out the stove. An army patrol drove past the top of the street. As Joe's feet touched the cold lino a shiver went through him.

'What's the time?' whispered Brendan.

'About half seven.'

'Oh God.'

He pulled his arm back inside the bed clothes and turned over.

'Give me a shout before you go, there's a good boy.'

'What for?'

'Ssssh,' said his brother and drifted back into sleep again.

'Will you eat an egg?'

'An egg?' His voice must have sounded surprised.

'Aye, an egg.'

'I'd eat an egg all right.'

She had the water boiling already and she slowly lowered a brown egg into it on a spoon. The water became calm for a moment and then foamed up almost to the top of the saucepan.

'Hard,' he said, watching her butter toast and cut the slices into little fingers. He was really getting the full treatment. 'I like them hard.'

'I know. Haven't I been feeding you eggs for years?'

Soft eggs.

The lid on the kettle rattled and she turned away to make the tea. He put a piece of the warm dribbling toast into his mouth.

'Friday today,' his mother said, almost gaily.

And he hadn't done his homework, let alone his extra homework. Eejit. Eejit.

'All day.' She put the pot on the table. 'Saturday tomorrow. It'll be nice to have a bit of a rest.'

'Are you ill?'

She smiled.

'No. I just get tired from time to time.'

'I suppose you would.'

'You can take it from me I do.'

She looked down at the egg, spoon in hand.

'It's cracked, I'm afraid.'

'That doesn't matter.'

She took it out and held it for a moment over the saucepan and then popped it into Joe's egg-cup. He watched the shell drying. A small ridge of white bubbled out along the crack. He hit the top with his spoon. His mother sighed. He looked up at her.

'Some people take holidays,' he suggested.

'Some people do indeed.' Her voice was bitter as the wind

could be. He pushed a piece of toast into his egg, which he saw with resignation wasn't as hard as it might have been. She took her cup of tea out of the kitchen and he could hear her in the front room rattling her sweeping brush against the legs of the chairs.

My mother is an obscure woman.

She won't speak the thoughts that are in her mind. She doesn't mean to be unkind. But sometimes she is.

She heard him starting to climb the stairs to wake Brendan.

'Where are you going?' she asked, coming into the kitchen with the brush in her hand.

'Brendan asked me to wake him before I went out.'

'I'll bring him a cup of tea in a few minutes. You get along to school.'

'What does he want waking for anyway?'

'Maybe he's going to get a job. First in the queue.'

'Maybe he is and maybe he isn't.'

The streets were full of soldiers. He passed two patrols on his way to school. Some walked backwards, they all turned constantly, their guns apparently casually looped through their arms, their hands and eyes tense. Joe always felt he couldn't run when they were about, had to walk with a casual air and measured steps as they did, in case he upset their balance of things.

It was a beautiful day with huge sailing clouds. Below in the river a ship hooted mournfully and seagulls floated on the wind just under the clouds. It was no day for school. The closed dusty windows, the dry air and the smell of Jimmy McCafferty's feet. No day for geometry.

A pigeon sat on the wall outside the classroom and picked unmentionable things out from under its wings with great enjoyment. Pick, fluff, burrow. Claws gripped on the stone coping. Pick, twitch.

'Joe Logan, what is the angle I have underlined? Do I disturb you? The name of the angle?'

'The angle . . .'

71

'Precisely.'

She re-underlined the angle fiercely. The chalk broke, giving him a moment's respite. As she stood up, slightly flushed from stooping, with the broken piece of chalk in her hand, she stared him straight in the eye.

'The angle?'

'Ob . . .' said Jimmy McCafferty out of the side of his mouth.

'Obscure,' said Joe, hopelessly.

Someone laughed.

She put the chalk down on her desk and dusted her hands on her tweed backside.

'Obtuse is the name of the angle, Joe Logan, and it is also the name for people the like of you.'

'I meant obtuse. The other word just slipped out. Honest I meant obtuse. The . . . other word has been running through my mind . . . you know . . .'

'I'm glad,' she said, with a menacing smile, 'to hear that something is running through your mind. More poetry, I presume.'

There was a long silence.

Bugger, he thought bitterly, why can't they ever leave you alone.

'Well?' Her voice was raised almost to shouting pitch.

'Something like that, miss. I'm sorry.'

The pigeon unfolded its wings and shivered.

'You will stay behind after school. In the meantime you will attend to the class. Obtuse is the word. Repeat it after me. Obtuse.'

'Obtuse.'

When he next looked out of the window the pigeon had gone. Bloody obtuse of it, he thought.

Kathleen was waiting for him when he came out. He saw her hunched figure on the wall as he came down the road, the familiar trail of smoke wisping away from her. He ran the last few yards. She looked up at him and smiled.

'Kept in again?'

He nodded.

'I thought I'd wait a while and see if you came.'

'Thanks.'

'It's a great evening.'

'Aye.'

'Tomorrow's Saturday.'

'All day.' He quoted his mother.

'I'd a sort of plan . . . if . . . well . . . you know . . . if . . .'

She dropped her cigarette butt on the pavement and squeezed it out with her toe. They started to walk along the road.

'If . . .?'

An army truck drove past. The soldier sitting on the back with his gun on his knee whistled at Kathleen. She paid no attention. The whistle annoyed him.

'If . . .?' he demanded.

'Oh yes. If you liked we might go up Grianan. I'd bring the food.'

He didn't answer.

'The weather might stay good. What do you think?'

'I thought you were cross with me'

'Cross?'

'Something like that. I just thought . . .' He looked past her at a leafless tree that waved at him across someone's wall, twiggy fingers trembling. He raised his hand in greeting and then blushed at his own foolishness. 'Well, I don't really mean cross . . .'

Their feet were in step, in, out, one, two, rhythm, down the steepening hill.

'I don't often get cross,' she said, considering the matter. 'I keep quiet and calm and terribly reasonable and then suddenly, whammm.' She waved her hand in the air flamboyantly. 'It's beyond crossness. Mad I get. You see cross women peering out from behind curtains . . . anyway, why would I be cross with you?'

'I don't know . . .'

'Let's forget whatever it was then. Tomorrow . . .?'

'Yes. That would be great. Smashing.'

He felt extreme excitement rising inside him like the froth rushing up in a bottle of coke that you've just given a great shaking.

The road widened and the crouching houses changed to rectangular blocks of flats, bleak, unwelcoming. Across the road the windows of the high flats were multicoloured with shining lights and above them again the street lights in the city were like small green flowers on their tall stalks.

'It's quiet,' he said.

'Thank God for small mercies.'

'Where are we walking to?'

'I don't know. Wherever our feet take us.'

He laughed.

A motorbike came down the hill behind them and puttered to a stop.

'Caught in the act.' Brendan's voice called from across the road. He was holding on to the back of a leather-coated friend.

'Oh, hello,' said Joe. He stopped walking and stared without enthusiasm at his brother. He was conscious of Kathleen beside him, her head slightly bent forward, her hand groping in her bag for her cigarettes. For a moment the two brothers were motionless, each one watching the other, animal-like, then Brendan turned to his friend and said something. The engine vroomed, slowly they moved off. Brendan raised a hand. Joe nodded. As he turned towards her she was lighting up.

'That was my brother.'

She shook the match and dropped it on the ground.

'Yes.'

'Brendan.'

They turned and their feet took them up the hill again.

'Do you know the other fellow?' she asked casually. 'The one he was with?'

'No.'

'He's not too good.'

'Oh.'

'You know what I mean?'

'It's nothing to do with me if he's good or bad.'

He shuffled his feet to get in step with her and they walked in silence for a couple of minutes.

'Would your parents mind if you came with me tomorrow?'

'Why would they mind?'

She looked briefly at his brave face and smiled.

'There's a bus at ten. We'll get the best of the day if we go early. I'll meet you at the depot.'

'That'll do.'

'Don't you worry about food.'

'Thanks.'

'Let's hope it doesn't rain.'

They were at the corner of his street. Light spilled on to the pavement from a lamp-post.

'Well . . .'

'Goodnight, Joe,' She said gently. 'We'll have a good time tomorrow.'

'Oh yes.'

He ran up the hill, leaning against the wind and taking little panting breaths that made his heart thump. Tomorrow, oh tomorrow. He said a quick prayer that Mam wouldn't be home before him, that the fire wouldn't be out, that Dad would be up in his stinking bed, that she would be in a good mood, that Brendan would keep his trap shut, oh God is it all too much to ask, and no rain, oh, please no rain, and I'll do my homework, I swear I will. Just for good measure he crossed his fingers, both hands.

'What kept you?'

She was stooped over the stove, rattling, when he went in. Her voice was fretful.

'I'll take the ashes out,' he offered.

Without a word she lifted the tray from under the stove

and walked out into the scullery with it held out stiffly in front of her.

Are you going to let me down God, all the way?

Above, his father's feet shuffled on the floor.

'I asked what kept you.'

She shoved the tray back into its place and wiped her hands on her overall.

He took a deep internal breath.

'We were arranging a day out tomorrow. To Grianan. One of the teachers . . .'

His voice died on him.

She picked up the coal hod and emptied it into the stove.

'One of the teachers . . .' he tried again.

She put a hand to her back and straightened up. She smiled at him.

'That'll be nice son. Grianan . . .' She sighed as she re-collected. 'Ah, Grianan . . . a lovely spot. A bit of air and a run around will do you the world of good.'

'Sit down, Mam, I'll make a cup of tea.'

He picked up the kettle and went out to the tap. Oh God, he prayed in the darkness, where's the harm? When he went back into the kitchen again she was standing by the table with her bag in her hand. She held out a coin towards him.

'You'll be needing money for the bus.'

Ah, Oh, God.

'Thank you.'

The door of his father's room opened and footsteps fumbled on the stairs.

'Put it away,' she said sharply to him, and moved with speed across the room to hide her bag in at the back of the press.

'Who were you with last night
Out in the pale moonlight?'

Brendan winked across the room at him as he sang. He had let a cold wind into the room with him as he entered,

76

which stirred the newspapers by Dad's chair. Joe squashed some strawberry jam down on to his bread and didn't look at his brother. His father slopped tea into his saucer as his shaking hand lifted the cup.

'Dum diddley um dum, dum, dum.'

There was a whiff of drink from him, and his eyes were shiny.

'You're late too. What's got into you both at all today?'

She got up slowly, pushing with her hands on her knees, and went over to get Brendan's plate out of the oven. Brendan winked again in the general direction of Joe and sat down. The legs of his chair squeaked over the linoleum. The strawberry jam was too sweet, it sickened the inside of Joe's mouth.

'It's all dried up,' said Mam, putting the plate down on the table in front of Brendan. 'But you've no one to blame but yourself.'

Father coughed. They had been told at school that seven million germs rushed out of your mouth when you coughed. Well, give or take a million or two. Probably several million more with the old fellow as he really put everything he had into his coughs. The strawberry jam would be a good germ trap. He put the half-eaten slice of bread down on the plate and pushed it away from him. Germ trap.

'Where were you anyway?' asked the old man, his coughing spasm past.

'Out and about. Celebrating.'

'It's well for you that has something to celebrate. There's not many in that position.' She handed a cup of tea across the table to him.

'There's no point in celebrating the end of one day even, because you know the next one is always there waiting for you.'

Brendan fumbled in his pocket for a moment and pulled out a fiver. He stretched it tight between his fingers. The Queen of England's face stared sternly up at him from the table. His father's eye was more than casually on the note.

77

'Would a fiver come in handy, Mam?'

He shoved it over to her. She let it lie by her plate.

'Where did you get that?' Her voice was sharp.

'Oh, the begrudger,' said father, his fingers visibly twitching.

'I've got a job.'

'Well now, isn't that grand?' said father. 'Isn't that grand. Did you hear that now?' He turned to his wife. 'Isn't that a great thing?'

There was silence.

'Didn't I say he'd do that? Didn't I tell you? Wasn't I right? By God, this calls for a celebration, so it does.' He looked hopefully at his son. Brendan gave him a wink and a nod. Intimate, almost secret.

'Are you not going to say anything, woman?'

'Aye. I'll say what I want to say, in my own time. No doubt, I'll have plenty to say.' The wind that blew across the Foyle in the winter was no colder than her voice.

'What's the job, Brendan?' asked Joe, as nobody else seemed to be going to ask that question.

'It's not much of a job, but it'll tide me over. Cash. It'll be a bit of cash. It's just driving stuff round for this fellow I met. He's in the import business. So he is. Like import, export. McKeady is his name. Mr McKeady. It's not much, just driving, but the money's not bad. It's a job for God's sake, Mam, isn't it?'

She picked the money up from the table and looked at it for a moment, then she put it into the pocket of her overall.

'The money'll come in handy, there's no denying that.'

There was a long pause.

'Thanks,' she said.

She leant over the table and touched his hand gently. He nodded briefly at her and moved his hand just out of her reach.

'My son will now assume the mantle of the breadwinner. Unlike his crippled father, he will win bread. What do you think of that, woman? My son will see us right. What do you say to that?'

She looked at him with contempt and said nothing.

'If looks could kill . . .' said the old man, raising a hand to protect himself.

'When do you start?' asked Joe.

'Monday.'

'That's great.'

'It's driving here and there, Mam. I may be away the odd night.'

'Yes,' was all she said.

The conversation fizzled out.

Knives and forks rattled and scraped. The father stooped to pick up the paper that he had dropped on the floor when Brendan had come into the house.

'Oooooh.' The breath groaned out of him as he reached down.

'Well, I must say I thought you'd all be pleased. Delirious. Sugar please.'

Joe passed the sugar bowl.

'I am delirious,' said the old man from behind his paper.

Joe felt a fit of laughter bursting up through his throat. He put a hand to his mouth to try and keep it from escaping.

'I'd rather you went back over there. You know that. I've said it over and over.'

'Ah Mam, for heaven's sake.'

'You never listen to me though.'

'You never talk sense, that's why.'

'I talk more sense than him.' She nodded towards the newspaper. It rattled indignantly.

'What's that? Sense is it? Isn't this the boy's own home? Hasn't he every right to live here if he wants to? If he so desires? And work. Ha. And see to things? And what do you do but complain when he puts five pounds into your hand? A nice thing that. My mother, God rest her, was no begrudger . . . no . . . I mind well the day I first put . . .'

'Would you stop. Just stop, that's all I ask. Take your

79

books on up to your room, Joe, and do your homework.'

'Tomorrow's Saturday . . .'

'Whisht, child. Away and do what you're told.'

He went slowly up the stairs, one heavy foot dragging
after the other. No one spoke. It was cold in his room and
there was nothing to do but get into bed. He didn't feel
like studying, so he lay in the dark, his school bag untouched
on the floor beside him, and the voices reached up to him,
full of anger and misunderstanding. He lay with his arms
folded back under his head and stared at the shimmering light
from the street as it coloured parts of his room. After the
voices grew into an explosion of words, the door slammed.
He could hear the men's feet climbing the steep street. He
could hear his mother crying. He put his hands over his ears
and turned his face into his pillow. 'Oh God,' he prayed.
'Don't let me grow up.'

He was awakened by Brendan coming into the room.
Even though he had taken off his shoes the soft shuffle of
his socks on the lino crept into Joe's head. He turned over
and opened his eyes. Outside, the sky was red. The room
was filled with the smell of smoke. He shut his eyes again
quickly and listened as his brother took off his clothes and
creaked into the big bed. The fire sirens were sounding.

'Joe.' It was a whisper.

The father was banging round in his room. The muttering of his voice could be heard through the wall.

'Joe.'

'Mmm?'

'Who was the bird?'

'Bird?'

Joe opened his eyes and looked at the light flickering on
the ceiling.

'What's burning?'

'The one you were with this afternoon. Who?'

'A teacher.'

God's holy truth.

'Yes, but, has she a fellow?'

80

Orange and black shapes twisted for a moment like dancers.

'A fellow?'

'Don't be bloody thick.'

'How would I know a thing like that?' He kept it to himself that she wore a ring, touched it from time to time with a gentle finger. 'I hardly know her anyway.'

'Oh.'

An army truck roared past the top of the road. A child cried for a moment next door. The ambulance clanged in the distance. Father coughed. Night music.

'Does she have a name?'

Why don't you leave it alone? She's my private life, my friend, my person.

'Doherty.'

'Miss Doherty?'

'Miss.'

That was all. He shut his eyes so tight the millions of dots whirled in his head and he fell asleep to the sound of the night music. Oh please God, oh God, oh blessed Mother of God don't let it rain tomorrow. Oh Kathleen . . . oh . . . friend . . . oh . . .

Mam never worked on Saturday, well, she didn't go out to work, to be more exact. It was the day she cleaned the house down from top to bottom, and boiled the towels and the dish cloths. Pans bubbled and steamed all morning on the stove, and she humped bucket after bucket of hot water up and down the stairs. The house was filled with the sound of her scrubbing brush working over the floors and banging against the walls, and also with the smell of soapy steam. By the end of the day her hands and the lower parts of her arms were red, and wrinkled like the nuts you see in the shops round Hallowe'en. She stripped the beds, and the pillow-cases and sheets were thrown into one of the bubbling buckets, and stirred and banged with a long wooden spoon, until they finally flapped wearily from the line in the back yard. Joe was glad to be leaving the house. Saturday was never a happy day. His mother's exertions, the draining of colour from her face as the day went on, the tight clamp of her hair on her forehead, the heavy burden her body seemed to become, made him uneasy. He always tried to keep out of her way, but she always wanted to know where he was going, who he was with, every moment of his time had to be accounted for.

She must have been up some time before him, as the buckets were all ready humming, on the stove. The long handle of the wooden spoon tapped gently against the side of one of them, keeping time with the vibration of the water as it bubbled.

'I've made you a drop of porridge. I thought it would stand to you.'

'Thanks.'

He sat down and felt guilty again about his half-lie, as he watched her spoon the porridge out into his bowl.

'There,' she said, as she put the bowl in front of him. 'That'll make your hair curl.'

It was one of her favourite sayings. He had tried once to make a poem out of it, but it had come to nothing.

'It's a good day for you anyway.'

He poured milk on to his porridge and watched it burrow its way underneath and then work its way up to the surface again.

'Mam . . .'

It was not the time for truth, she was peering into one of the buckets, poking with irritation at whatever it was that bubbled inside.

'Mmmm' She was indifferent to anything he might want to say.

'Oh, nothing.'

'Don't go and get your clothes ruined, mucking about.'

The sugar that lay on the porridge was gritty and he crunched it off the spoon with pleasure.

'Did you hear me, son?'

'Aye.'

'Well, mind me.'

'Aye. I will.'

> Gold is the sun
> On a winter's morning.
> Cold is the air.
> Still is the river
> On a winter's morning.
> The hill beyond is black
> Against the gold sun.

Hurry, hurry. The day waking, waving golden flags across the sky. Down the dry streets, still smoke-smelling. Past the eyeless houses, people resting still behind the cardboard windows. Soldiers watchful at street corners. Eyes in the backs of their heads. Seagulls mew, dip and soar, watchful like the waiting soldiers, but free.

She was standing by the bus waiting for him. The cigarette stuck in one corner of her mouth was unlit, her hands were clenched, warming in her pockets, a large red shopping bag hung from her shoulder. She was staring with a slight frown through the wire fence that protected the gardening shop, at some brightly painted gnomes. She looked as if she thought he wouldn't turn up.

'Hello,' he said, alarmed suddenly by the thought of the day stretching ahead. What will we say to each other, he wondered with panic.

She turned and smiled.

'Hi, there.' She spoke with a phoney American accent that made him smile. 'Would you like a gnome for your birthday?' She took the cigarette out of her mouth and looked at it for a moment.

'What would I do with a gnome?'

'Look, I haven't a match. I don't suppose you have a match?'

He shook his head. 'What a stupid question for me to ask anyway. Of course you wouldn't have a match. I'll just

83

dash round the corner and get some. I'm desperate for a smoke. Don't let the driver go without me. Here.' She shoved a ticket into his hand.

'I have money,' he said, with a certain pride.

'It's my party.'

She was off through the checkpoint, one of the soldiers whistling after her as she went.

The driver was writing something in a little black book. He didn't look as if he were thinking of leaving immediately. Joe looked at the gnomes. There were four of them, each one playing a different musical instrument. There were flower pots and urns and a dry fountain, and a whole lot of sacks with writing on them that he couldn't read. Someone had told him that this shop had been blown up more times than any other shop in the city. He wondered why. Some people who didn't like gnomes perhaps? I'd like a fountain, he thought, a splashing towering one, with basin on top of basin, water bubbling in the air and falling, shining down from basin to basin. He smiled to think of the hens in the yard next door scratching and chooking to the sound of his fountain. A man came to the door of the prefab that stood where the garden shop used to be and looked at Joe looking at the fountain. He seemed to see what was in Joe's mind and smiled and went back into the shop again.

'Dreamtime,' said Kathleen in his ear. He jumped.

'Oh.'

Behind them the driver had stopped writing in his book and was revving the engine.

'It might have gone without us,' she said, almost severely, as they got on board.

'Never.'

They went upstairs so that they could see over the walls and hedges and into people's gardens.

'I love the double-deckers.'

He settled himself down happily and rubbed the smeary mist off the inside of the window with the sleeve of his

84

anorak. Kathleen put a cigarette into her mouth and lit it.
She took a deep breath of poison.

'Aaah.'

'You'll never learn.'

'Too right.'

The bus backed slowly out of the bomb site and started
up the hill. There were no other passengers on the top.

'We're off,' said Kathleen.

At the top of the hill they could see the river bending
away, curling along the broad valley towards the sea. A
driving wind churned the water.

'Do you like boats?' she asked.

He shrugged.

'I like looking at them. I've never . . . I wouldn't want . . .'

Houses hid the river. The gardens they could see across
the walls were winter-brown, biding their time.

Below, someone turned on a transistor and the music
drifted up to them. It made everything rather gay.

'Will I tell you a poem I wrote?'

'That would be nice.'

She bent slightly towards him so that she could catch
every word he spoke, as if it were important. He liked that.
She had a good listening face. He spoke with confidence.

'Gold is the sun
On a winter's morning.
Cold is the air.
Still is the river
On a winter's morning.
The hill beyond is black
Against the gold sun.'

There was silence between them as she waited for more.

'You don't have to rhyme,' he explained.

'Oh, I know.' She smiled at him. 'It's very short. I like it.
I'd like more of it.'

'That's the way it came into my mind'

'It's nice. A sort of picture really.'

'It's a present for you.'

He blushed and turned quickly to look out of the window.

'I . . . mean . . . I'll write it down and give it to you . . . if . . . well, you know.'

'I would like that very much, Joe. No one has ever given me such a lovely present before.'

'Ah, go on.'

The top of a double-decker bus is a beautiful place to be. You rock rather than roll along, getting a giraffe's-eye view into other people's lives and over the straggling hedges that normally hide the countryside from sight. At the checkpoint before the border a soldier clattered up the stairs, his gun crooked into his elbow. Kathleen opened the shopping bag and held it out towards him.

He rummaged.

'Ta love.'

He looked at Joe and grinned.

'Got any dangerous weapons on you, mate?'

Joe shook his head.

'Lost your tongue?'

'No.'

'One of the silent types.'

The bus vibrated under them. The soldier didn't seem in any hurry to go.

'Is he your brother then?'

'No,' said Kathleen gravely. 'Just a friend.'

'Bit young, ent he, for a girl like you?'

'Maybe he's older then he looks. Maybe,' she suggested, 'he's ninety-three. Or is it ninety-four, granddad?'

'Ninety-seven on Sunday,' said Joe, his voice crackling with old age.

'Just a couple of fruit and nut cases,' said the soldier, and went down the stairs again, dangerous weapons clanking and creaking all over him. They laughed. Joe looked out of the window as the soldier stepped down on to the road. He looked up at them and waved. Joe didn't wave back. Kathleen hesitated a moment and then as the bus began to move she leant across him and flapped her hand against the glass.

'Why?' asked Joe.

She touched her ring nervously before she answered.

'I don't suppose he exactly likes being here, any more than we . . . He's a kid. Something like that . . . Do you think he knows what he's doing here?'

'I've heard them coming in the night . . .'

'I know. I know.'

The bus lurched over the ramps . . . Brown hills rose up from the sides of the valley and, on ahead, misty blue mountains.

'I feel the way you do too, most of the time, but then I know . . . I know really . . . they're not all bad. Like I said, kids. I know there are the toughies too. I saw one in a pub in Belfast one night crying because he wanted to go home.'

Joe thought about that.

'Mind you, he was drunk . . . but nevertheless.'

'Yes,' said Joe. 'Drunks do cry.'

'They usually mean what they're crying about. We may find it boring or funny even, but it's tragedy to them.'

'Tragedy.' He thought about his father for a moment. She nudged his arm. 'Here we are. This is where we get out.'

They got up and swayed to the top of the stairs. As they were going carefully down, the bus gave an energetic leap sideways round the corner which nearly threw them one on top of the other out on to the road.

'Hey,' said Joe, alarmed for a moment.

'Hey. Hey.'

The bus stopped and they got out, each a little red in the face.

A few houses were scattered along the sides of the road, a bar, a bicycle shop and an old railway station house with unused level crossing gates, now rusted shut. The wind thrummed gaily through the telegraph wires above their heads. Kathleen hitched her bag firmly on to her shoulder and set off up a narrow road with high tattered hedges on either side. She walked with a swing in her movements, like a real country girl, he thought, placing each foot with confidence on the stony road. Her stride was longer than his, and he had almost to run to keep beside her.

'It's a good step,' she said, nodding up the hill ahead of them. 'But it'll do neither of us any harm.'

'You're not from Derry, are you?'

'I've only been here a couple of years. My parents would turn in their narrow graves if they knew where I was.'

'Why?'

'That was a silly thing to say. I don't think they'd really mind. Worry. They'd worry. They were never too keen on the North. Like a lot of people down there. They looked on the border as a sort of necessary protection. Keeping out some awful plague.' She sighed. 'They were simple people. Nice. Very nice when you look back on them.'

Through a gate he could see long brown fields stretching below them. Rooks pecked through the furrows fastidiously. Away in the distance lay the shine of water. The tree-tops were flattened by eternal wind.

'Nice.' She repeated the word, aware of its inadequacy. 'But hopeless people.'

He didn't like to ask the question that was first in his mind.

'Where did they live?' he asked instead.

'Wicklow.'

'Oh.'

It meant little to him. Just a name from a page in a book. Green shading on a map.

'On a clear day you can see Wales from the top of the hill behind the village. Quite clear. Big blue mountains.' She spoke with pride.

'Wales.'

'Yes.'

'That must be nice.'

She laughed.

'I don't know why I told you really. I always used to hope I'd see Wales when I got to the top. Another world.

Like outer space or something. Am I walking too fast for you?'

'Well . . .'

She slowed down, groping as she did so in her pocket for the cigarettes and matches.

'My father had the only pub in Ireland that never made any money. My mother was a teacher. I get my brains from her and my bad habits from him.'

'Have you many of them?'

'Oodles of brains.'

'I meant bad habits.'

She laughed.

'More oodles.'

What happened to them? Joe only asked the question inside his head. What happened to nice people? He had a picture of a nice small man polishing glasses, his head only just appearing over the top of a high bar counter. It was one of those slightly comical bald heads that looked as if an expensive yellow duster were used on it morning and evening. Ragged cuffs on his shirt because he had no money to buy new ones and his wife was too busy teaching to mend his old ones. She was talking. The vibrations of her voice reached into his mind, but not the words. Soon the twiggy branches of the hedges would start to burst with green, he would like to come again then. Sharp green. Soft unfolding leaves, acid colour that you could almost taste in your mouth when you thought about it. The vibrations became words. He looked towards her. Her cheeks were pink with the wind in her face and her hair blew straight out behind her like a cracking flag.

'She was always saying to him, there's other people on the road, Jack, besides yourself, and he would laugh and say he'd few pleasures in life and that was one of them and not to be nagging like other men's wives did and if she didn't like it she could get out and walk and she'd laugh and say, don't say I didn't warn you, and I suppose that was how it happened.'

She paused for a moment and then gave one of her little laughs. 'He was what the Americans would call a speed merchant.'

'Oh.'

'They never got old anyway. There's something to be said for that. He had gorgeous teeth.'

'What happened to the pub?'

'My cousin has it. He'd been working in England for ages. He always knew he'd come into it some day. He was married. They came back.'

They walked in silence for a moment.

'They put their savings into the place. Did it up. Carpets and that sort of thing. A juke box. Changed the name from Dohertys to The Hill Top Lounge. Snacks, car park and music on Saturday night. People come in cars. There's a very beautiful view.'

'Wales?'

She shook her head.

'No. Not Wales. I don't go back.'

She stopped walking and put a cigarette into her mouth. Carefully holding the match box in her sheltering hand, she struck a match and bent her head down to catch the flame.

'My memories are so . . . I don't know . . . clean . . . clear . . . that's not quite right . . . oh dear me, Joe, I'm as stupid as hell.' She dropped the dead match on the ground and moved on up the road. Her deprecating laugh was blown back to him by the wind. He hurried his steps to keep up with her. His cheeks and nose were feeling wind-stung.

'I talk too much. To myself all the time. Inside talking and outside talking. To converse with yourself is a very satisfactory thing to do. To argue with yourself, philosophise, laugh at your own rotten jokes . . . If you were five or six years older you'd tell me to shut up, so you would.'

'I like it when you talk.'

'Thanks, pal.'

The road turned sharply to the right and the hill became

steeper. Trees hung across the hedge on the upper side of the road, some of them already with tiny thickenings on the winter twigs that would become buds. Smoke waved from the chimney of a small cottage tucked below the road. The smell of turf-smoke filled the wind. A black and white dog came round the corner of the cottage and inspected them without interest . . . Away below, the silver fingers of the lough grasped at the fields. The windows of a distant village across the valley glittered in the sun.

'Chocolate?'

She pulled a bar out of her pocket and handed it to him.

'Thanks.'

It was a long walk. It took them in fact the best part of an hour to reach the top. The trees and hedges ended and the world unfolded itself below them. The wind pushed and pulled at them from all angles. The last couple of hundred yards to the high stone ring was up a winding track. It seemed as if they might be blown whirling away for ever if they didn't watch out, keep their feet gripping firmly to the ground. They tucked their heads well down into their shoulders and ran the last few yards to the shelter of the fort.

'Oooof.'

There was a low dark passage that smelt disagreeably of pee and then they were in the fort.

'It's supposed to be two thousand years old,' said Kathleen.

The walls rose high around them in tiers, each tier joined by stone steps that jutted out from the wall. There was no breath of wind but they could hear it battering outside.

'Did people live here?'

The circle of grass was like a huge circus ring. Small holes at intervals round the wall led into tunnels.

'I imagine only in times of danger. They used to rush up here with their cattle and throw stones at the marauders.'

'True?'

'More or less. Come on up here.'

She began to climb cautiously up the steps.

'Just a tick.'

He went over to one of the holes and, bending down, put his head in. There was a passage there all right, a sort of crawling passage. He wondered if he were brave enough to crawl along it a bit. After all, he thought, if it had been there for two thousand years it would be unlikely to fall in on top of him. It was damp and very dark and very uninviting. He wriggled a short way along it, his body completely blocking out the light. There was a smell he didn't like. A smell that might be of dead things, dead things he might put his hand on at any minute. He backed quickly out into the light again. He wiped his hands carefully on his trousers. His heart was stuttering in his chest.

'Thick idiot.'

He said the words aloud. He crouched down and forced himself to look in again. Something moved in the darkness. He got up in what he hoped was a casual way and looked around for Kathleen. She was up on the top of the fort leaning over the wall.

'Come on up,' she yelled down at him. 'Up.' The wind took the word from her mouth and tossed it away towards the gathering clouds.

'Up.'

She waved at him with both hands. Her hair and all her clothes were filled with wind and seemed to dance. He began to climb the steps, carefully fitting his feet on to the odd-shaped stones. He reached the first tier and looked down into the circus ring, seeing in his mind's eye the small people crouched round their fires, the frightened cattle trampling people to death, and clashing round them with their huge horns.

'They couldn't have,' he shouted up at Kathleen.

'Couldn't have what?'

'They couldn't have had the cattle in here with them.'

She shrugged and turned back to the view. He climbed up the next set of steps and joined her.

'There wouldn't have been room.'

'I'm only saying what I've been told. But look, if the wind doesn't blow you away, you can see four counties. So they say.'

The whole world swung beneath them. The fortress city was below them, its grey walls and climbing houses quite plain to be seen, in the crook of the curling river which broadened then into the lough, beyond which the cliff of Benevenagh rose like a wall. Across Inishowen shadows moved constantly over the surface of Lough Swilly making it look as if it were alive with creatures of different colours and shapes. Away beyond, divided from each other by brown hills Mulroy Bay and Sheephaven glittered and the great mountains of Errigal and Muckish rose above the rest, rising blue from the treeless boglands and rimming them along the Atlantic ocean, a silver line between the earth and sky. Storm clouds were banking up in the west, grey and white and sun-shot as if the sea was boiling up into the sky. Then back from the loughs and the sea the mountains subsided into hills again, and the bog became tilled winter fields neatly patterning the land, and trees waited and smoke blew bravely from the cottage chimneys, and the river Foyle again wound its way along its valley from Strabane to pro-tect its own city. It was as if he owned the world.

'Oh,' was all he could say, but he needn't have bothered as the wind pushed the exclamation back down his throat again.

So he walked around the walls in silence, and again and again, pushing his way against the wind, clutching from time to time protectively at his hair. The clouds gathered round Errigal, and as he watched, the distant mountain was quite hidden, as if it had never existed. If he could write a poem. Now, but now. But nothing came into his head except the drumming of the wind. It was a long time before he realised that Kathleen was no longer up there. He looked down into the fort and saw her hunched against the wall, smoking furiously.

He climbed with care down the steps and walked across the grass to her. Large raindrops burst on the side of his face. He looked up, above the walls the sky was blue, the sun was still shining.

'Another monkey's wedding.'

'Monkeys are being married all the time. Quick into the gateway or we'll be drowned.'

The day suddenly turned from blue to black and rain came tumbling out of the sky. They stood in the darkness and watched it and tried not to notice the bitter smell from the stones on the ground.

'Food,' she said. 'I'm frozen. I can't think how you were able to stay up there so long.'

He realised as she spoke that he was frozen too.

'It was so . . .' His jaws had become stiff. He rubbed at them with his hands, trying to get them back into working order. '. . . so . . . massive.'

She nodded. She took a plastic bag out of her shopping bag and handed it to him.

'Here. That's your share. I should have brought something hot to drink, but I didn't. Eat up though. It'll warm you a bit.'

They leant against the damp wall and munched. They munched cold sausages and ham sandwiches, egg sandwiches and lovely salty corned beef sandwiches. She obviously took picnics seriously. The rain continued to pour down and small streams began to trickle through the stones around their feet.

'Oh dear,' she said. 'Oh help,' and dropped a sandwich. He bent to pick it up.

'Ugh, no. Leave it. I wouldn't want to eat anything that had been on this bit of ground. Polluted, I would say.'

'Have one of mine?' He hoped she wouldn't, he was ravenous. She shook her head.

'No thanks. I'll have another dangerous cigarette . . . Then we can warm ourselves around the match.'

He laughed.

94

'Your face is purple.'

'It's nothing to what yours is, with bits of boiled egg stuck to it.'

He rubbed at his chin with the back of his hand.

'Is it ever going to let up?'

He went over to the doorway and peered out. It was now almost impossible to see more than a hundred yards, the rain and the clouds were the same heavy grey.

'It's going to rain forever. This will be the only safe place for miles around. They'll all be rowing out here in their boats in a couple of days.'

'And we'll be here to welcome them. Hot drinks and fires in the bedrooms.'

'I've never had a fire in my bedroom.' Behind the press there was a tiny black fireplace. He had found it one day when he was looking for a penny that had been trying to escape.

'It's the nicest thing in the world. I only ever had one if I was sick. Just to lie there and watch the flickering patterns on the ceiling.'

He laughed abruptly.

'I can do that anyway.'

'Oh damn,' she said.

'Well,' she said, after a long silence. 'There are two alternatives, we can run now and get soaked, or we can wait.'

'What's the point in waiting?'

'The rain might slacken off.'

'A man with a big umbrella might appear.'

'The world might come to an end.'

'We'll freeze if we stay here much longer.'

'O.K. So. We'll run.'

She set off down the track, stones skittering out from under her feet as she ran, her bag thumping against her back. Her hands clutched her coat together at the throat. Joe followed. Black water streamed everywhere, raced around their feet, filled his school shoes. Nothing in the world was dry and calm.

Once they were on the road there was some shelter from the gusts of wind, but none from the rain. They ran for nearly a mile and then their running became slower and slower, turning finally into an ungainly shuffle, hardly quicker than walking and far more painful.

'Ooh hoo. Oooh hoo,' panted Kathleen.

'I'm warm anyway,' said Joe. He felt as if steam should be rising in clouds from his body. 'Will we have long to wait for a bus?'

'Don't let's even discuss it. A quick prayer is our only hope.'

They were lucky. As they reached the main road they saw a bus bumping towards them past the level crossing gates.

'Oh stop, please stop.'

They ran. Kathleen waved her arms in despair. Joe waved his arms and put on a pathetic face. The bus obligingly slowed down and then stopped in a great wash of muddy water. They ran across the road and climbed on.

'Have youse been swumming?'

The driver took the money from Kathleen's dripping hand.

'Quack, quack.'

'Quock.' He handed her the change.

They didn't bother going upstairs, but sat in drowned silence staring out of the window at the rain and feeling the wetness creeping through them to their bones.

'I get stitches,' said Joe after a while.

'They pass,' said Kathleen, pulling at the ends of her hair with her fingers. 'Was that a disaster?' She asked eventually.

'Oh no. It was great. A great place. I'd love to go back.' He laughed. 'Not now. It was . . . well . . . I felt like God up there.'

'Mmmm.'

'It'd be great to be God living up there. Sort of organising things. Rain here, a bit more wind blowing there. A storm, a raging storm. Thunder and lightning. Wham.'

'What about some sun, God?'

'Only for the goodies.'

'I'm glad you're not God. Tell you what, we'll go back to my room when we get off the bus and hang all our clothes around the fire and have something hot. Hot. I'm sure your mother'll have a fit if you go home like that.'

'That'd be great.'

'Sure?'

He nodded.

They jolted past the garages and small factories built along the side of the road. The few shops had their lights on. There were practically no people in the streets. An army truck passed them. The soldiers in the back, balancing their rifles on their knees, wore capes that were shining with wetness.

'Know something?'

'What?'

'It must be over two hours since you had a cigarette.'

'Oh, you monster.'

As the bus drew into the bomb site Joe saw Brendan standing by the corner of the garden shop. He looked quickly away and edged himself behind Kathleen as she stepped down from the bus.

'Quock,' said the driver behind them, as he wrote down the time of their arrival on a card.

Kathleen burst into one of her laughs. Joe tucked his head down between his shoulders and stared at the ground. If he couldn't see Brendan, perhaps Brendan couldn't see him. The ostrich principle.

'Hello.'

He heard Kathleen's voice tentatively speaking.

'Hello, Miss . . .' Brendan hesitated.

The ostrich never wins.

'Hello, Brendan,' he said, trying not to sound too unfriendly.

'Hi, kiddo.'

The three of them stood for a moment looking uncertainly at each other.

'Quock, quock.' The driver jumped down from the bus and nudged Kathleen with his elbow as he passed.

'You're wet,' commented Brendan finally. 'The two of you.'

'You are, too.' Kathleen put out a hand and touched his sleeve. 'Have you been waiting for us?'

'Well . . . sort of . . . Miss . . . Miss . . . ?'

'Doherty,' said Joe, without much enthusiasm.

'Oh, call me Kathleen.'

Brendan nodded thanks at her.

'There's been a bit of trouble . . . well, you know . . . bother . . . nothing too bad, but Mam asked me to see he got safely home. The wain.'

Bloody cheek, thought Joe. Lies, too. I bet that's a lie. The wain. He looked at Kathleen who was looking at Brendan as if he were an honest, good-hearted sort of person.

'We thought we'd go to my place and dry off a bit. Your mother wouldn't mind that, would she?'

'I don't suppose she would.'

Liar. Cheat. Finagler.

'That's good. Why don't you come too and have a cup of tea?' She looked a bit embarrassed suddenly. 'I mean . . . you don't have to . . . or anything . . . I can see Joe home. Safely. Just if you've nothing else . . .'

'Right on,' said Brendan.

They started to walk up the hill. The rain was easing off.

'What was the trouble? Was anyone hurt?'

'There was rioting in Waterloo Street. This morning.'

'Bad?'

'Quite bad. A couple of shops went. The usual sort of thing.'

'Anyone hurt?'

'Not too bad.' He paused for a moment. 'A couple of soldiers killed.'

'Oh, God.' Joe's legs had stiffened after the bus ride and

98

he was having trouble in getting himself up the hill.

'How?'

'Shot. Sniper. Single-shot killings. Marksman stuff.'

'You sound pleased.'

'I won't weep any tears. Will you?'

'You could spend all your life crying.'

'Hasn't your job started yet?' asked Joe.

'Monday. I'll be away for five days on Monday. That make you happy?'

Joe scowled.

'What's your new job?'

'Just driving. Long-distance lorry. You know.'

'Over to England and back?'

'Well, no. Just round and about. Across the border and that. No great shakes.'

'Will you like that?'

'Beggars can't be choosers, Miss . . . um . . . Doherty.'

'Kathleen.'

'Twist my arm, Kathleen.'

Joe stamped suddenly in a large muddy puddle and dirty water splashed them all.

'Hey,' said Brendan.

'Sorry,' said Joe.

'Oh, Joe, you are careless. Lucky I'm soaking already,' said Kathleen.

'Sorry,' said Joe.

'Look where you're putting your big feet, kiddo.'

'I said sorry, didn't I?'

'What do you teach. Joe?'

She laughed.

'I don't teach Joe anything. I teach sweet little girls.'

'Oh, I . . .'

'Joe and I picked each other up in the street. Didn't we, Joe?'

'He has good taste for a kid.'

She looked pleased.

Joe considered stamping in another puddle but decided

that only anger and misunderstanding would be achieved by such a gesture. He thought instead of the pale fingers of water and how distant rain seemed to form a pillar between the land and sky holding up the turbulent clouds.

They turned a corner and the wind hurled rain and grit into their faces and the heavy smell of wet smoke. The road was littered with stones and broken bottles and some fragments of window glass. A couple of houses had rags stuffed in their tattered windows which struggled furiously in the wind trying to escape. Kathleen took Joe's hand and they ran across the road, picking their way through the debris. Brendan's feet shuffled behind. If only the wind would blow him away. Whoosh, no more shuffling feet, no more Brendan. How I would love you, wind.

The hall in Kathleen's house seemed slightly warmer than the street. The mutter of a television set came from behind one of the closed doors. Kathleen ran up the stairs in front of them.

'You'll have to wait on the landing while I change out of my wet clothes. I'll only be a tick.'

She went into her room and shut the door. Joe could hear her moving inside the room, pulling the curtains, the click of the electric switch, the scrape of a chair along the floor. Two scenery paintings in gold frames and four grey doors were the only things to stare at, unless he stared at Brendan. Joe moved to one of the pictures. Some sheep browsed through some very purple heather and blue mountains made patterns in the background. He could see from where he stood that the other picture was much the same. There was no sound from behind any of the other doors, presumably the occupants of the rooms were either dead or out. The carpet had triangular blue patterns on a red background, most of which had been walked off by years of feet, leaving just naked string.

He tried to will his eyes to see through the door in front of him, see the tables and chairs, the divan, the gas fire, the personal belongings that lay around.

'You'll catch a cold.' Brendan's voice interfered with his concentration.

'What?'

'You'll catch a cold standing around in those wet clothes.

Joe began to dance. He toed and heeled around the landing like a prize winner. He waved his arms above his head like a puppet on a string. The floor trembled under him.

Brendan watched him for a couple of minutes.

'What do you think you're at?' His face was lined with irritation.

'I'm warming my blood.' He sang the words to the dancing tune that was running in his head.

'War . . . arm . . . ing my blooood.'

'For God's sake, Joe. Sometimes I think you're a bit thick. Wanting.'

'Well, I'm not. If anyone's thick it's you. You . . . ou . . . ou.'

'You'll have someone up.'

Kathleen opened her door. She was dressed in a long, red woolly dressing-gown. She had rubbed at her hair with a towel and it was sticking out round her head in mad tangles. She laughed when she saw Joe.

'Poor boy. Is it that bad? Come on in quick.'

They followed her into the room. The fire was glowing and already the kettle was making its first stirring noises. She handed Joe a dark brown coat.

'Here. Take this down to the bathroom and get out of all your wet clothes. All.'

'I'll be all right.'

'Do what you're told.' Her voice was surprisingly sharp. The schoolteacher. Joe went out again on to the cold landing. He stamped his way down four steps to the bathroom and turned the handle. The door was locked. Someone was in there. He could hear the slight splash and slither of water in the bath.

'Hump.'

He went back up to the landing again. He could hear her

laughing through the door. Brendan must have said something funny. Mind you, she laughed easily. Maybe it was one of her own jokes she was laughing at. Brendan's low voice broke into her laughter. Joe took off his anorak and dropped it on the floor. Then his jersey and his shirt. Even his vest was wet. It had holes all round the bottom where he kept pulling it down and his fingers had worn their way through the woolly material. It was cold. The person in the bathroom turned on the tap again. Joe put on the coat, its lining was slithery and made him shiver. It reached almost down to his ankles.

Kathleen laughed again.

'Women,' he grunted aloud, as he bent down to remove his sodden shoes, 'are all the same.'

He didn't quite know what he meant by the remark, but it gave him a small satisfaction to say the words. After the shoe, his socks went on to the pile. Then his jeans came off and, in the one operation, his pants hidden inside them. He was now naked under the coat, which he buttoned carefully from neck to knee. A right eejit. He picked up his clothes and opened the door.

'That was quick,' said Kathleen. 'Shut the door and don't let the heat out.'

She took his clothes from him and festooned them like Christmas decorations round the fire. Steam began to rise from them, and the smell of wet wool. Brendan was sitting in the armchair, his legs stretched out in front of him, as if he owned the place. The kettle whistled cheerfully.

'Give your head a rub with the towel, Joe.'

She poured some water from the kettle into the teapot, and clasping it in both of her hands she rocked it backwards and forwards for a few moments before emptying it out into the basin. She measured the tea into the pot and then poured more water in on top.

'Would you make me some toast, Joe?'

She moved across the room with the teapot and put it down carefully in front of the fire.

'Here.'

She picked up a small metal toasting fork that was leaning against the chimney and pulled the two ends. The fork
grew as Joe watched.

'What's that?' he asked.

'A toasting fork.'

She handed it to him. He pushed the ends together and
then pulled them apart again.

'That's a great gadget.'

She put a sliced loaf in its red and white wrapping down
on the floor beside him.

'Make lots,' she said. 'I'm starving.'

Joe balanced the first piece of bread on the three prongs
of the fork and held it out towards the fire. The warmth
came up the fork and along his arm through the old brown
coat to his naked body. Oh. The bread curled inwards
slightly with the heat from the fire. The warmth moved
through him as a person moves around a room, touching
objects here and there with careful fingers. He looked at the
bread, the near side to the fire was just beginning to colour.

The fire was glowing evenly all over. Reliable.

The sea holds the land

With care in its hand.

Long fingers reach

Far in and greedily try to steal

Green fields.

A voice.

'Joe.'

Her voice.

'Oh . . . ah . . . what?'

'The toast.'

Smoke.

'Oh dear.'

He pulled the charred bread off the fork.

'I'm sorry.'

'Just watch what you're doing,' said his brother.

'You must have gone asleep,' said Kathleen. She was

pushing sausages round in the pan. There was a beautiful smell of frying.

'No. I wasn't asleep. I was just . . .' He blushed. She took the burnt toast from his hand.

'You must be tired, after all that walking and running and weather.'

He put another piece of bread on the fork.

'Better luck next time.'

He made six perfect pieces of toast and Brendan buttered each one as it was ready and put it on a plate in front of the fire. The butter made golden pools on the toast as it melted.

'There we are now.'

Kathleen put a plate full of sausages and baked beans on to Joe's knee. Brendan poured out three mugs of dark brown tea and they all sat as close as they could to the fire and munched in silence, surrounded by the steaming clothes. The wind tried hard enough but couldn't get through the window to join them.

'That was great.' They were the first words Brendan had spoken for a long time. He put his plate on the floor beside him and patted his stomach with what Joe considered to be a rather vulgar gesture.

'I would like to give you something, so I would. That's made a new man of me. Something in return.'

'What about a cigarette, perhaps?'

'I've noticed you smoke too much.'

'That's what Joe says too.'

He pulled a packet out of his pocket and threw them over to her.

'Thanks.'

'But that's not what I meant. I thought I'd give you something . . . well . . . like a kiss, or a song, or a promise.'

Joe, who had the last bite of sausage in his mouth, almost choked with anger. He looked sideways at Kathleen's face. He might have known it, she was laughing. So was Brendan, in a sheepish sort of way. Joe picked up the toasting fork and pulled it in and out distractedly. It made a slight squeaking, complaining sound.

'Are you any good at singing?'

Maybe, thought Joe, she hadn't heard the first outrageous suggestion.

'Not bad. Joe'll tell you.'

'Well, Joe? How's his singing?'

'Not bad,' said Joe almost inaudibly.

'A song then. That would be nice.'

She settled herself on the floor, in a serious listening position. The light from the fire glittered in her drying hair. She let the unlit cigarette droop between the fingers of her right hand. She gave a quick warm smile at Brendan.

'Fire ahead.'

'What would you like?'

'I'm not choosing. You have to do that. That's part of the whole thing.'

Brendan chewed thoughtfully at his thumbnail.

'I'd like to give you a present too,' said Joe.

'But you have. You gave me that poem. It's been a lovely day for presents. If you put a hand into that drawer beside you, you'll find a pen and some paper, then you could write it down for me.'

'A poem?' Brendan spoke without removing his thumb. He looked like a small, surprised child.

'A poem,' said Kathleen gravely. 'You get on with choosing your song and leave Joe and his poem alone.'

Joe balanced the writing pad on his knee and began to write. He would make a pattern on the page with the words, he thought.

Brendan sat up straight in his chair and took his thumb out of his mouth.

'Are you ready?'

'On tenterhooks.'

He shut his eyes and began to sing.

'If I were a blackbird
I'd whistle and sing,

And I'd follow the ship
That my true love was in,
And on the top rigging
I'd there build my nest,
And I'd pillow my head
On his snowy white breast.'

After the first couple of nervous lines he sang nicely. Kathleen listened with care. The clothes steamed. Joe pressed black furrows of writing on to the page. He tried to block out the words of the song with the words of the poem. Rhythms and rhymes became confused in his head. He got the words down on the paper, black and fierce-looking and tried to think of another verse.

'I am a young maiden,
My story is sad.
For once I was loved
By a young sailor lad.'

Words and thoughts jumbled in his head, but nothing would come out the way he wanted. Neat words on the page. Coherence. Neat thought. Everything's spoilt, a voice kept saying. The whole day, spoilt. Life, perhaps, spoilt. Never again will the words come out neatly. Never again will I see pictures in my mind. Tears rose to the back of his eyes. My bloody brother is a bloody Provo. He wrote the words in deep black writing across the page. Spoiling the page. She didn't want his bloody rubbishy poem anyway. He tore the paper from the pad and began folding it into eight little concertina folds, over and back, over and back. He ran his nail along each fold, inflicting private injury. He was suddenly aware of silence. Only a slight ticking from the gas fire sounded in the room.

That was lovely. Really lovely. Thank you, Brendan.'

'You really think so.'

'You have a gorgeous voice. I never thought for a minute you'd be able to sing as well as that. Doesn't he sing beautifully, Joe?'

Joe leaned towards the fire, arm outstretched, and lit the

106

end of the paper. He held it out over the grate, watching the paper curl under as it burned, glowing, then turning black and floating down to the floor like feathers.

'Yes.'

'Who did you get your voice from? Your mother or your father?'

'My father was a great singer before . . .'

'Before what?'

'Ah, well . . . when he was younger. He's an old man now. His voice is old. Shook. You know.'

'Are you trying to set the house on fire, Joe?'

He shook his head.

'Have you my poem written out for me?'

'I couldn't remember it.'

'Oh, Joe . . .' Her voice was full of reproach for the lie he was telling.

'Do you write poetry, Joe?'

Brendan got up as he spoke and went over to Kathleen. He lit a match and held it down to her.

'You'll have that cigarette ruined if you don't smoke it, twisting and twiddling at it like that.'

'Thanks.' She leaned forward and the tiny flame of the match made a golden flicker across her face for a moment.

'He wrote me a poem anyway. A very nice one too. I'm sure you'll remember it if you try. Please try.'

She leant towards him and touched his knee with the tip of her finger.

'Yes, I will. I'll write it out at home.'

'Good boy. I loved my day. Rain and all. Didn't you love it, Joe?'

'Yes.'

'Were you ever up there, Brendan?'

'No.'

'You must go sometime. It's like being on top of the world. You could fly.'

'I've never had the urge. I've looked at it, but . . . I like streets.'

'A city boy. All the same, when the weather gets better you should go. Just to have a look.'

'Did you know the song I sang?'

'My father used to sing it. He didn't have a voice like you though. He used to crack on the high notes.'

'I think,' said Joe, 'we should go home. Mam will be wondering where we are.'

Kathleen put out a hand and felt his jersey.

'Your clothes won't be nearly dry yet.'

'No matter. I think . . .' He got up from the floor, holding the coat carefully round him.

'Ah, sit down, kiddo, and stop fussing.'

Kathleen got up and began to gather his clothes together.

'Yes. You'd better go. I wouldn't want your mother to be upset.'

'Oh, God,' said Brendan. 'Everyone's fussing.'

She handed Joe his clothes.

'Do you want to take them down to the bathroom.'

'Someone's in there. Having a bath.'

'They'll be out by now. Our bathroom's not a place to linger.'

'I'll stay here, just the same.'

'Suit yourself.'

His clothes were still damp, but warm rather than cold damp. He knew that the moment he went out into the wind they would chill him as they had before. He wriggled into them under the long coat. He'd seen his mother once on the beach wriggling into her clothes under a long striped towel, desperately clutching at the corners with her fingers.

'Fuss, fuss.' Brendan stretched his legs out towards the fire, not wanting to go.

'Leave him be,' said Kathleen.

'Would you come out with me one evening? Have a jar or go to a dance or something? Somewhere decent, you know?'

She thought about it.

'Would you?'

'That would be nice.'

Joe had his pants and trousers on. He slowly unbuttoned the coat and dropped it on to the back of a chair. He pulled his vest over his head, tugging it down as far as he could over his white body. His vest, at least, was dry, and smelt companionably of his own body.

'I don't know when I'll be back, but I could drop round here and we'll fix something.'

'You could do that.'

'You wouldn't mind?'

She laughed.

'Why would I mind?'

'Well . . .'

'Don't be silly. You sound as if you'd never asked a girl out before.'

He reddened and grinned.

'Maybe I haven't.'

'Don't give me that one.'

She's my friend. That's what she is. He buttoned up his shirt with clumsy fingers. Not girl friend. Friend. Just that . . . and he has to go and stick his nose in. Oh hahahaha. And I can't even write a poem down on a piece of paper. Oh hahahaha. He pulled his jersey over his head. He had to struggle to get his head through the tight neck. As always, there was the thought of suffocation, a panic, over when the eyes and nose got free.

'You're still soaking.' She felt his arm anxiously. 'You'd better get home as quickly as you can and change out of those clothes.'

The landing was cold. The bathroom was still occupied as they passed it. He pointed out the thin line of light under the door to Kathleen.

'Saturday's bath day,' she said. 'They're all queueing up with their flannels and soap.'

'We don't have a bath at home.'

'You must come and join the queue some day.'

They laughed and Joe felt better.

'I'll write out that poem for you. I'll see you after school.'
'You're a love.'
She opened the door and the wind pulled at their clothes and punched their faces.
'Quick, go. Fly. We mustn't let too much of that in.'
'Goodbye and thanks. It was great.'
'Yes. We'll do it again.'
'I'll be in touch,' said Brendan.
'Goodbye.' She shut the door and they hurried off down the hill.
'What did you have to say that for?' asked Brendan.
'What?'
'That, about us not having a bathroom.'
'It's true. We haven't.'
'No need to spread it around. Not to . . . well, not to spread it around.'
'In future I'll tell everyone we've two bathrooms with fitted carpets and telly.'
'There's no need to be bloody cheeky.'

'When Brendan's away, can I go back in my own bed again?'
Monday. That awful morning. Homework not finished. Winter sunshine trying to edge its way through net curtains. Ashes and dust still blowing through the tired streets. Mam's face full of pain at having to move into yet another week. He could hear Brendan moving upstairs and the pan sizzled with a fry for the working man.
'You'll stay where you are.'
'Ah, Mam . . .'
'I spoke,' she said sharply. 'I spoke and that's that. I have enough trouble on me without you causing me more. There's nothing wrong with the bed you're in. There's many has no bed.'
'But that's my bed he's in. It isn't fair.'
'Will you quit. Just quit.' She spooned some fat over the egg in the pan. He visualised the face of the egg turning

from yellow to faintest pink. 'Life isn't fair and it's time you knew it.'

He swallowed down a mouthful of tea and got up from the table.

'Finish your toast.'

She had eyes in the back of her head.

'I've had enough.'

She slammed the spoon down on the top of the stove, but said nothing. He picked his school bag up from the floor and left the room.

'Goodbye,' he said, as he reached the door. She didn't reply. Brendan was in the passage, stuffing things into his duffel bag. He was wearing a black leather jacket and tight blue jeans.

'Off to school?'

Joe nodded as he pushed past him and took down his coat.

'Look, kiddo, I'm sorry if I muscled in on Saturday. Did I spoil your crack? Did I?'

'I didn't care. Why should I?'

'Here.' Brendan held a fifty-pence piece out towards his brother. 'Could you use this?'

'Thanks.' Joe took the coin.

'See you in a few days. Be good. Tooraloo.' He went in to the kitchen to have his pink egg and bacon crisp and curled around the edges. He would remain untouched by Mam's anger. Joe banged the door as he went out.

During the maths class he wrote out the poem for Kathleen. He used the centre page of his exercise book so that he could pull it out neatly without anyone noticing. Miss McCabe paid no heed to him for the whole class. No questions were flung in his direction. The mysteries of diameter and radius passed over and around him.

Taking into account the mood his mother had been in in the morning, he decided it would be best to go straight home and not loiter around looking for Kathleen. He hoped, though, that he might see her on his way. There was no sign of her. The girls were all over the place, in their protective, nudging groups, seeing and yet not seeing the boys. She must have stayed behind to speak severely to someone, or have a word with the head, or, maybe, just to chat with a friend. He faintly disliked the thought of her having friends. He preferred the picture of her as a brooding solitary, alone, except for her moments with him. That made him feel good. His feet did a little shuffling dance on the pavement, and a girl from one of the groups whistled at him. He walked from then on with composure.

He was almost at the top of his road when he heard his name. He stopped and looked round. She was waving to him from outside the sweet shop.

'Hey.'

He went back towards her.

'Hello.'

A passing car suddenly put its lights on, like some sort of salute. It was that no man's land time of evening, without colour.

'I saw you pass.'

She waved a box of cigarettes in front of his face.

'You never heard me. You looked asleep. Sleep-walking. Were you writing a poem?'

He smiled.

'Here.'

He took the neatly folded paper out of his pocket and handed it to her. She opened her bag and put it inside, tucking it tidily into one of those narrow pockets that always seem to be in bags, useless pockets, unless people give you poems from time to time.

'Thank you. I'm glad you remembered it.'

They started to walk back the way Joe had been going.

'I hope you didn't get into trouble on Saturday.'

'Oh no . . . you see . . .' he blushed. '. . . She thought I was with the school. So . . .' He gestured his mother's resignation with his hands.

'I do believe you are a villain.'

112

He nodded, pleased at the word she used. At his corner they stopped.

'I must get home,' he said.

'Yes.'

'I'll maybe see you tomorrow.'

She shook her head.

'We have exams all this week. I'll be frantic. I am frantic. Come round on Friday. Come and have tea, why don't you?'

'Aye. I'd like that.'

'Good. See you then. How's Brendan?'

'He's away.'

He went down the hill. After a few yards he turned and looked back at her. She was standing where he had left her struggling to protect a flickering match. It went out. She dropped it on the ground and started again.

'You'll be dead before you're forty,' he called to her.

She straightened up and put the unlit cigarette back in the box, and the box back in her pocket.

'Since when have you become the voice of my conscience. Go away and do your homework and leave me to my vices in peace.'

It was the way it had always been before Brendan had come home.

'Is that you, Joe?'

The voice crackled down the stair full of exhausted anger.

'It's me. I'll be up to you in a minute.'

He rattled out the ashes and filled the stove. He put on the kettle and then carried the bucket of ashes out to the yard. It was dark and bitterly cold. The wind drove needles of rain along the valley between the houses. Not even the hens next door made a sound.

'Chook,' said Joe, hopefully. There was no reaction from the hens. His father was thumping on the floor with his stick.

'I'll be up when I've made the tea.'

The thumping continued until he arrived up in the room with the steaming cup in his hand.

'Did you let it draw?'

'Yes.'

'It doesn't look as if you let it draw. No one could drink that muck.'

He pushed the cup away, slopping tea over Joe's fingers. Joe put the cup down on the table and wiped his fingers on his trousers.

'It's muck if you don't let it draw. Everyone knows that.'

'You were banging . . .'

'Of course, it's my fault. I might have known.'

'Ah, Dadda . . .'

'Where's your brother?'

'He's away. You know that. He's on a job now. A driving job.'

'I've been alone all day. There's been no one to see to me at all.'

'Well . . .'

'Where's Brendan?'

'I told you. He's away on a job.'

'I've been bad. He's the only one sees to me at all. He takes me out to meet his friends. They listen to me. Yes. They talk. They tell me things. Is he doing a job for the Movement?'

'He's got a job driving for someone. That's all I know. It's a business of some sort.'

'A business . . . ha ha. That's a good one. You could call it a business all right.

'I only know what he told me.'

'He tells me, so he does. My own son. I was head of a flying column once. Did you know that?'

'You told me.'

'You want to go, don't you? Get away off to your books or the T.V.? I see it in your face. Get on away then. I'll just lie here on my own till Brendan gets back.'

'He'll be away a few days.'

'She's even lifted the shoes on me. I've looked everywhere for them. The bloody bitch.'

'Sure, you don't need your shoes. Your slippers are here.' Joe picked them up from under the bed and handed them to his father, who swept them away with his hand as he had swept away the cup of tea.

'It's my shoes I need, I tell you. Have a look below for me. I haven't looked below. It'd be like her to take them to work with her, to spite me she'd do a thing like that.'

'Dad . . .'

'Shoes, I tell you.'

Joe went down the stairs and looked around the kitchen for his father's shoes. He found them quite quickly, tucked tidily into the space between the dresser and the wall, covered with a couple of copies of the *Journal*. He considered the situation and decided it would be preferable in the long run to let his father have his shoes now, quickly, so that he could be off and out with a bit of luck before Mam came in. He ran up the stairs and threw the shoes on to his father's bed.

'There's your shoes.'

The man on the bed appeared to have dropped off into an uncomfortable sleep. He grunted, but made no movement. Joe slipped out of the room and went down and settled himself to his homework. As he sat down he heard the bed begin to creak and the rasp of his father's breathing as he bent down to push the shoes on to his feet and fumble with the laces. He did the whole job remarkably quickly, and then his footsteps shuffled across the floor and down the stairs.

'I'm away out. I have a few old friends to meet.' He paused in the doorway. 'After all . . .' He was panting with the exertions he had just been through. 'After all . . . friends . . . I'll not be missed here anyway.' His hand went with pride to his pocket. 'My son gave me the wherewithal. Yes.'

He closed the door and Joe could hear him feeling his way along the passage. There was a sudden sharp laugh.

'The wherewithal.'
The door slammed.

He must have spent the wherewithal in one savage go as he was laid flat on his back until Brendan came home on Thursday evening and they both went out together and didn't come home until all hours.

'I'll not be back for tea,' said Joe to the back of his mother's head on Friday morning. She turned and looked at him.

'Why? What are you up to?'

'A couple of us are going to Logues for tea. Mrs Logue said we could. We have work to do. One of those project things.'

The words came out of his mouth too quickly. Under the table the fingers of both his hands were crossed and squeezed together. Her face was suspicious. 'We're going to have a game of football first.' Weaving a tissue of lies. He uncrossed the fingers on one hand and took a large mouthful of toast. He chewed toast and lies and jam all together, watching her anxiously.

'I won't have you staying out late.' Her voice was doubtful.

'Miss McCabe says Jimmy Logue is better at maths than I am.'

That wasn't a lie anyway.

'She says it would be good if someone gave me a hand, from time to time, with my maths.'

'It's Miss McCabe's job to do that.'

'She hasn't the time. She's worked half to death. Jimmy's great at maths.'

There was silence between them. Upstairs his father called out suddenly, nothing in particular, just a sudden cry in his sleep.

'Will you be home by eight if I let you go?'

His heart lifted.

'Ooh yes, Mam.'

'And don't be playing out in the street after it's dark. And don't be going near any trouble. They're good people, the Logues. You can go this once anyway.'

'Thanks, Mam.'

That was that.

'How was Brendan's job?'

'I don't know, son. He was in and out like a dose of salts, taking your Daddy with him. I never saw them again, thank God. He seemed happy enough. He gave me a few pound to keep me quiet.' She laughed sharply. 'That's all that matters, the few pound. I'm not complaining and I'm not making any enquiries either.'

He sat on the wall waiting for Kathleen to arrive.

'Spring might come soon.'

She had come up behind him and put a hand on his shoulder.

'I really feel it might. Last week I thought we were stuck in winter for ever. You can smell the river.'

He sniffed.

'I can't.'

'You must have a rotten nose.'

'My nose is O.K.'

'Not if you can't smell spring coming.'

He sniffed again.

'Dust and smoke. That's all.'

'And you say you're a poet.'

'I have to be home by eight,' he said, as they reached her door.

'That's all right. I'll walk round with you.'

'You needn't bother.'

'It's no bother. I'd like to and I'm sure your mother would want me to.'

She bent down and lit the fire.

'There now. The room'll warm up in a few minutes. I thought we'd have fried chicken and chips. Is that all right?'

'Great.'

'Well, sit down and talk to me while I get on with it.'

'How are the exams going?'

'That we won't talk about. I have mountains of papers to correct. I hate it. I hate it. I'll be delighted to give the whole thing up. Shoving useless bits of information into the young and innocent.'

She took a knife out of a drawer and began to cut up an onion. The smell reached over to Joe and made his nose twitch. Nothing wrong with that nose. 'Are you going to give it up?'

'Yes. Here anyway. At the end of this year.'

'What'll you do then?'

'Oh hoohooh oooh.' Tears were pouring down her cheeks. 'They always make me cry.' She pushed at the onions with her thumb. 'I hope you like them, otherwise I'm torturing myself for nothing.'

'Fried?'

'Yes.'

'Right on. What are you going to do?'

'I'm going to England.'

'Why ever?'

She dumped the onion rings in the pan and turned on the tap. She held her hands under the running water, watching the water hit them and splay off into the basin. After a few moments she smelled them carefully and then dried them on the dish cloth.

'You have to have an open mind,' she said. 'I'm not a very rooted person. I could live anywhere. At least I think I could. You've got to get along with people. That's important. That's all part of having an open mind. I love Ireland . . . a sort of earth love . . . rather than anything else. I don't feel committed to teach Ireland's snotty-nosed young. English snotty-nosed young will do me just as well. Or Chinese, if it comes to that.'

She stirred the onions vigorously with a wooden spoon. He thought about what she had said.

'I might travel about a bit,' he said, eventually.

'You might.'

'I don't know though. I can't see how I'd ever get out of here.'

'You have to want to, then it's easy. I'm getting married, so it's very easy.'

'Oh.'

There was a very long silence. At least that put a stop to Brendan's carrying on.

'That'll be nice."

'I hope so.'

'I don't think I'll ever get married.'

'You're very pessimistic this evening. Of course you will.'

'I don't think I want to.'

'You'll probably change your mind when you grow up. Anyway, if you're going to be a poet you'll have all the girls in Ireland chasing you, and you won't be able to resist the temptation.'

'What's his name?'

'Fred. A very boring name. I keep asking him to change it, but he won't.'

'Oh.'

'Fred Burgess, so I will be Mrs Burgess. How do you like that?'

'It's O.K.'

He tried to see in his head what someone called Fred Burgess would look like. He'd have to be fat, he thought, but he got no further than that. She had changed for him. She was no longer one of those solitary people like himself. Even her face seemed to be changed by what she had told him.

'He's a soldier.' She said the words abruptly. She put the wooden spoon down on the edge of the pan and came over to Joe. She pulled nervously at his hair. 'So he is. I'm telling you because you're my pal. He's in Germany and I'm lonely. You'd like him. Honestly, you would. His mother came from Cork and . . . oh . . . Joe . . .' He looked up at her and was

119

suddenly aware of how unhappy she was. He took her hand and rubbed at the finger that wore the ring. He couldn't think of anything to say. She put the other hand up suddenly to her face, so that he shouldn't see her crying eyes.

'I shouldn't have come here. I see that now . . . I thought . . . I didn't understand before I came . . . no one can understand . . . I thought it would be a good thing to do. But I feel so awful . . . God . . .'

She rubbed at the tears with her thumb and a smile pulled at one corner of her mouth.

'It's no wonder I smoke so much.'

'It's O.K.' said Joe. 'It's honestly O.K.'

'Why have I bothered you?'

'The onions are burning.'

She began to laugh through her tears. Another monkey's wedding.

'Oh, hell. I am the champion messer of the world.'

She scrabbled at the onions with the spoon.

'I like them burnt,' said Joe helpfully.

'It's just as well.'

She scooped them on to a plate and put them into the tiny oven.

'I wasn't cut out to be a good cook. I don't quite know what I was cut out to be. I get carried away by my own emotions. I am purposeless.'

'What does that mean?'

'I suppose I don't know what I'm at . . . and mind. Lots of people don't know and they don't mind. I mind. I'd like to know where . . . be sure of something. Even how to cook onions.'

'You're going to get married.'

She sighed.

'I suppose so. That's not purpose though. It's sort of routine really. The birth, marriage, death routine.'

'Why are you doing it then?'

'It's hard to explain about love, even to yourself. And

then . . . I hate living on my own . . . you need someone . . . I just wish I'd never come to Derry.'

'I'm glad you did.'

'Thank you, Joe.'

She held the pan under the tap and let a stream of hot water run on to it.

Steam enveloped her for a moment.

'You'll have to come and stay with us. You know, when all this is over. When you're older.'

'All what?' he asked, and then remembered. 'Oh, Yes.'

'We're going to live in Germany for the first while. That'll be nice, won't it?'

'Yes.'

'I'm looking forward to it.'

He wished she'd stop talking. She shouldn't be unhappy. The safe people should never be unhappy. It was too shattering. The bitterness of his mother and father he could manage. Some confidence inside himself told him that he would never be like that. But that life should gnaw at her in this way made him feel uneasy. As she had said, she bothered him. It was all most unfair. Suddenly she began to sing. Her movements by the cooker were neat and organised, in spite of what she said about herself. Her hands moved with composure, unlike his mother's heavy movements as she cooked.

Now we have time to kill,
Kill the shadows on our skin.
Kill the fire that burns within
Killing time, my friend.

'That's the song you liked, isn't it?'

He nodded.

'I'm afraid I don't sing as well as Brendan.'

'My Dad's the one.'

'A singer as well as a hero.'

'Hero.' Joe's voice was bitter. 'Mauryah.'

She laughed.

'We all hate our parents some time in our lives. And

sometimes we're sad about it later on and sometimes we're not. I don't suppose it matters much. It's all just part of the routine too.'

She went on singing. He wondered if she realised that it eased his thoughts.

The strange rhythm of the song broke the clotted sadness in his head.

'Would you kill anyone? Any . . . you know . . . person?'

'How can you ever tell the answer to that one? I wouldn't want to kill anyone, and I think if I ever did kill anyone, for whatever reason, it would probably be the wrong thing to do.'

There was a long silence. Only the sight of the gas fire whispering through the room.

'I wouldn't.' He spoke fiercely. 'I wouldn't. No matter what.'

'Ah, pet . . .'

He didn't like that and frowned slightly.

'Joe . . . Sometimes we're not able to help the things that happen to us. The things we do. We have no control . . . at times, that is. It's easier to think the right thoughts than to do the right things.'

'I wouldn't,' he repeated.

She started to sing softly again, there being no answer to that.

Kill flying time before it rushes past
Catch in your hand the moments you love most.

The words grew in his head against the rhythm of the song.

Kill flying time,
Move slower to the grave.

Prolong . . . he was stuck. Prolong this moment. This warmth, these words that we throw between each other. He felt the stinging rush of tears up behind his eyes and put his head back to make things difficult for them. He hummed the song with her.

122

'There you are,' she said. 'You don't sing badly at all.'

He hit the bridge of his nose sharply with the hard edge of his fingers and brought the tears jumping out on to his cheeks.

'Ow,' he said, without meaning to.

'What did you do that for?'

'I just did it.'

He mopped up his face with his sleeve and grinned at her.

'You are a funny fellow.'

'Funny?'

'Clown.'

'I saw a circus once. There used to be circuses here, before . . . The clowns were great. Mad. Falling about. Blowing themselves up and things. I remember . . .'

'What?'

'Oh, the noise. Bangs and that. And the smell.'

'Elephant piss and sawdust.'

He started to laugh.

'Something like that.'

'Here.' She handed him a plate piled high with chicken and brown crunchy chips and the burnt onions.

The plate was hot and the heat wore its way through his trousers and was uncomfortable on his legs for a few minutes and then became the most pleasant warmth in the world and then became a memory.

'I must go. It's getting on for eight.'

The floor between them was littered with plates and mugs. He picked his way carefully through the debris.

'I'll come with you.'

'There's no need. Honestly.'

'I'd feel better if I did.'

'I don't want you to.'

'Too bad.'

They put their coats on in silence and went down the stairs in silence and out of the door. Rain had settled in for the evening, a fine drenching rain, that seemed to spread itself under your clothes.

'There'll be no trouble tonight,' he said to her on the doorstep.

'Joe, I'm walking to the top of your road with you and that's that.' It was the schoolteacher voice again.

There wasn't a soul in the streets. The houses seemed to huddle even closer together in an effort to keep dry.

'You're all right here. Good night, Joe.'

'Good night . . . and thanks a lot.'

'See you soon. Oy . . . Joe . . .'

'Yes?'

'Don't say a word about what I told you.'

'About?'

'You know what about. Fred and all that. Silent, O Moyle. Right?'

'Right. Good night.'

'Good night.'

You could go on saying good night for ever, he thought, as he ran down the hill.

Brendan was back when he got in. The table had been cleared of the tea things and the two men sat, one on each side of the table, their heads stuck into the newspapers. Mam was darning his grey socks. She held the sock close up to her eyes. It was stretched over a wooden mushroom that had belonged to her mother before her. The needle dipped in and out of the wool, making its neat pattern. Her fingers looked old, the skin creased like unironed clothes. Joe joined them at the table.

'Hi, kiddo.'

'You're back.'

'I'm back.'

'Did you have a good evening, son?' She raised her eyes from the sock. Her hands were still for a moment.

'Aye.' His voice was non-committal.

'Where were you?' Brendan folded up the paper as he spoke.

For one dreadful moment Joe couldn't remember where
he had told his mother he had been going. His face must
have shown his panic, because Brendan got up from the
table and tapped him on the head with the folded newspaper.

'I was over at Logues.' He spoke the words quickly and
quietly in case his mother thought to cross-examine him
about his evening. What did you have for your tea?
and what had Mrs Logue to say for herself and this and
that? But she was busy pulling at a piece of grey wool
with her teeth, the sock in one hand, the needle in the
other.

'I'm away out,' said Brendan to all and sundry.

His father dropped the paper on the floor.

'I'll be with you.'

'Not tonight, Dad. I have a fella to see.'

The old man pushed himself up on to his feet.

'I'll not be in your way. Your friends are my friends. I
can keep a deaf ear if I have to. We can have a mouthful
of beer.'

'No, Dad . . . not tonight . . . It's work I have . . .'

'I'll wait up in the bar till you've finished your work.'

'Sorry.'

Without waiting for any more discussion, Brendan turned
and left the room. The three of them waited in silence until
the hall door had closed. Mam moved first. She put the
sock on its mushroom down on the table.

'I'll make a cup of tea.'

She got up and went out to the scullery.

The old man sat down slowly in his chair.

'He's never done that to me before.'

Joe stared at the squares on the oilcloth. Some crumbs
still remained from their tea.

'He never . . .'

Joe could hear the water running into the kettle and
then the squeak the tap always made when it was turned
off.

'Weeks he's been home now and he's never gone without me.'

'There's a first time for everything.'

She carried the kettle in and put it on the stove.

'His friends were my friends.'

'Can't you leave him be. There's no other boy in Derry had to take his old father around with him wherever he went. Making a show of him.'

'They were always glad to see me, so they were . . . Always listened. Always engaged me in edifying conversation. They had time for me.'

'Well, tonight they'll have a bit of peace.'

'You're hard.'

'It's better to be hard than soft in the head.'

There was no reply to that one . . . The old man's head drooped towards his chest. Some small worm of pity moved inside Joe.

'Maybe he has a girl,' he said and was instantly appalled by the words, by the possibility of the truth in the words, by the possibility . . .

'A girl.' His mother spoke with alarm. 'Is that true?'

'Wouldn't I know if he had a girl? Haven't I the boy's confidence?' His head had come up and he watched Joe's face with care.

'It was only a suggestion,' muttered Joe.

'Have you seen him with a girl?' asked his mother.

'How could he see him with a girl when he hasn't a girl?'

'Will you shut your mouth for a minute. Joe?'

'No, I haven't.' God forgive me, I am becoming a truly hardened liar.

'What did I say?' The father was triumphant. 'No word of a girl has ever passed his lips.'

The kettle sighed for a moment and then was silent again.

'No word. And all the talk out of him.'

'I wonder who she is.'

'Mam, I didn't really mean it. I only said it . . .

'Sure, why wouldn't he have a girl. It's a perfectly natural thing for a young man his age.'

'I would have advised agin it.'

'You would?' Her voice was ironic.

'Aye. I would. No point in getting mixed up with girls when you're in the Movement. I know to my bitterness.'

She didn't answer. She put the teapot down on the stove and poured some hot water into it. She carried the pot in her cupped hands out to the scullery.

'You and your Movement.'

She disappeared into the darkness. The water from the pot splashed into the sink.

'I would have advised agin it. And let me tell you, the boy would have listened to me. His father.'

He would go and visit her. Stay. And Frederick. Fred. He might stay for ages. He could grow up there. He could learn to watch the world as she did. Fred would take off his uniform when he came home and you could forget what he was. He would be a man, like any other man. They would be careful of each other, and gentle, and laugh. He saw the ring, that she touched from time to time, on her finger. Remembered the way she touched it. I would like to be loved, he thought. Safely loved. To write words down on a page, pattern them not even write them down, hear the song of them in your head, hear nothing else for those few minutes, that was safe too. He might stay for ever. He might buy a typewriter. Those neat black letters looked so good. Some day Maybe they would live in Germany. He tried to remember what he knew about Germany. Pine trees and deep snow in the winter, keeping the world silent. She would have children of her own. She wouldn't want him hanging around. He could help, push them in their pram. Teach them games like conkers and hopscotch and making shadows on the wall with your hands. Our Father who art in heaven, please . . . Hallowed . . . hallow was a lovely word . . . Hallowed be Thy . . .'

'Are you deaf?'

'What?'

His tea was on the table in front of him and his mother was sitting once more in her chair with the sock in her hand. She was staring at him.

'Sorry,' he said. He didn't quite know why.

'Drink your tea while it's hot.'

'Yes.'

'I sometimes think you're a little wanting.'

'Ah, Mam . . .'

'Three times I ask you a question and you just sit there like a gaum.'

'I was thinking.'

His father seemed to have gone asleep. His head was right down on his chest, his eyes were shut. He too was ignoring the tea that steamed in front of him.

'What did you ask me? I'm sorry.'

'About the girl . . .'

'I know nothing about a girl, Mam. I only said it off the top of my head. Something to say. You took me up. That's all. You took me up.'

'Aye' breathed the old man across the table. 'You took him up.'

'Drink your tea.' Squinting up towards the light she threaded her needle and continued with her darning.

It was late when Brendan came in, long after closing time. Joe had lain awake, not because he wanted to, but because sleep wouldn't come. He had listened to his parents getting themselves to their beds, the shufflings and creakings, the little grunts and moans that people make as they do the normal things of life, the sounds they are never aware of themselves. The clink of glass on glass in his father's room, the rattle of springs. The interminable rise and fall of his mother's voice as she prayed. She would have a hole worn in the floor by her bed one of these days. Footsteps from time to time in the street, brisk on the wet pavement, people making their way as fast as they could from one place to another, heads pulled down inside protecting collars, their faces shining like the streets with the smear of rain. It was strange, he thought, that at night you could even hear the furniture make breathing noises. There was no such a thing as silence, and you only became aware of this at night.

He didn't hear Brendan's steps approaching the house. The first thing he heard was the creaking of the stairs and then the sound of the door opening slowly. Through a crack in his eyes Joe watched his brother drop his clothes on to the floor and climb naked into bed. That would drive Mam wild if she ever found out. She hated that. To her, it was sinful as well as unhygienic.

'Joe.' A whisper.

'Are you awake?'

Joe didn't answer.

Brendan sighed and then turned over and in a few minutes began to snore.

Brendan woke up the next morning as Joe was dressing. He put a white arm out from under the bedclothes and touched the window pane. There was a hopeful glitter of sun on the glass.

'A good day for a drive.' He folded his arms across his chest, outside the blankets, and stared at the ceiling.

'If you had a car.'

'I have.'

'Go on.'

'I have the loan of one. For the day.'

'Oh.'

'What's the time?'

'Getting on for nine.'

Brendan yawned and stretched his arms above his head.

'That's a nice girl.'

'Who do you mean?'

'You know well who I mean.'

'I'm taking her for a drive today.'

'Did you ask her?'

'Of course I asked her. I went round there last night before I went to meet the boys. She was just clearing up after you.'

Joe felt his face getting red.

'She made me a cup of tea.'

'And you asked her?'

'For God's sake, Joe, are you thick or something? I asked her and she said yes . . . If you want to know she said she'd be delighted.'

'Can I come?'

'No.'

'Why not?'

'I said no.'

'Please Brendan.'

'No.'

There was a long pause.

'Why not?'

'Because I want to have a good time. And I won't have a good time with you playing gooseberry in the back seat.'

'She's my friend.'

'Don't you want her to enjoy herself?'

'Yes, of course.'

'Then shut up.'

'I hope it rains. Pours. And you run out of petrol and get a puncture.' He went out of the room and slammed the door.

'What was all that about?' asked Mam from her usual Saturday morning position by the stove.

'All what?'

'All that yelling and door-banging?'

'Nothing.'

'There's enough trouble in this house without you and Brendan fighting. Did you bring me down your dirty clothes?'

'No.'

'Then go and get them, and Brendan's while you're at it.'

It was a horrible Saturday. Brendan went out without a word to anyone, whistling as he clattered down the stairs and out the hall door. The house quivered with the cleaning it was getting. Joe seemed permanently in the way. There was trouble in the city and she wouldn't let him go out. His father never left his bed and she had Joe running up and down the stairs with trays and papers and angry messages all morning.

'Run up and tell your Daddy to turn the radio down. My head is splitting with the noise of it.'

Fed up. And the sun was shining with summer brilliance, showing up the dirty streaks on the windows and the grey cracked paint.

'Run up with a cup of tea for your Daddy and see if he's alive at all.'

Bored. He could see in his mind the sun on the lough and the leafless trees bending in the wind and hear her light laugh blown away with cigarette smoke.

'Bring me down the pillow slips from your Daddy's room and tell him it's time he got up.'

Bone-bored.

He wondered what sort of a car Brendan had borrowed. He had once seen a sleek blue bomb of a car sliding down the Strand Road, with curving silver horns, like dragon's heads. It wouldn't be one like that anyway. That was for sure.

'How did you get your shirt so dirty this week? It's like a rag.'

There wasn't even a cloud in the sky.

At about three his mother was out in the yard, flapping the sheets to remove the creases and folding them over her arm before hanging them on the line. There was a knock on the door. It was his friend Peter on the step.

'Coming out?'

'She wouldn't let me.'

Peter took a strip of gum from his pocket and shoved it into his mouth and held another one out to Joe. Joe took it.

They both chewed as they considered the situation.

'Don't ask her,' advised Peter eventually.

The hell with it.

Joe looked behind him down the passage. There was no sign of her. He reached up to the hook behind the door and took down his anorak. He closed the door quietly behind him and they ran hell for leather down the street. Well out of her reach they stopped, pink in the face and panting.

'Why wouldn't she let you out?'

Joe jerked his head in the direction of the hill. There was little menace in the sounds of shouting that reached them. The blueness of the day laid a carefree veil over the city. A lovely day for a bit of rioting. The best for months.

'Let's go and see what they're up to.'

Peter's voice had the wish for action in it.

Joe shook his head.

'You go on down if you want to.'

'Ah come on. Where's the harm?'

'It's the row . . .'

'Aren't you in for a row anyway? Come on. It's something to do.'

'What's on at the pictures?'

'I don't want to go to the pictures.'

Peter spat his ball of gum into the gutter and put another one into his mouth.

'We can't just stand here all day.'

He moved away from Joe, experimentally, towards the promise of fun. Unwillingly Joe followed. At the top of William Street they stopped and looked down the long sweep of the hill. The sharp smell of burning caught in their noses. Down across the bottom of the street people were running and they could hear the thwunk of rubber bullets. Peter looked back at Joe. The motion of his chewing jaws made him seem as if he were talking internally to himself.

'Well, I'm not going down there, that's for sure,' said Joe.

'Mmm.'

'Are you?'

There was the wail of an ambulance siren. Two Saracens turned into the street just below them and moved down towards the crowd.

'Hear that?'

Joe nodded.

'I saw a fella once hit in the eye with a rubber bullet. Did I tell you?'

'Yes,' said Joe. 'You told me.'

'I think I'll not go down either.'

'No.'

'It might get bad.'

'Yes.'

Peter turned his back on the fighting and leaned his head confidentially towards Joe.

'To tell the truth, my Mam doesn't . . . well, you know . . .'

'Yes.' They both stared at each other and chewed, relieved by the need for caution.

'She gets scared.'

'I know. Mine's the same.'

'She thinks I might get hurted.'

'Yes.'

'Or something.'

'Yes.'

'I reckon there's a lot feel like that.'

'I suppose so.'

'What'll we do?'

They began to walk slowly back the way they had come.

'I haven't a clue.'

'Will you come back with me and we'll watch TV?'

'Might as well.'

Crack. The sound was near and easily identifiable. The boys walked a little faster.

'It's getting cold,' said Peter. He pulled up the hood of his anorak.

'It is,' agreed Joe.

'That wasn't a rubber bullet.'
'It was not.'

Joe got home about a quarter to six. He hung up his coat and went into the kitchen. The table was laid for tea. There was no sign of his father. His mother sat across the table, leaning once more over her darning. She got up as he came in, putting her work down carefully on the table. She didn't say a word. She made sure with her fingers that the needle was safely threaded into the sock and then she walked round the table to where Joe was standing. She lifted her right hand and slapped him hard across the face. Then she turned and went back to her seat again.

'Don't you dare ever do that sort of thing on me again . . .'
Her voice was matter of fact, hardly even angry. She picked up the darning. He stood looking at her through the splinters of tears in his eyes. He put up a hand and touched his face.

'You've probably broken my jaw,' he said eventually.
'No,' she said, 'I haven't, but I will the next time. Sit down now, like a good boy, and I'll get you your tea when I finish this sock.'

'I wish you'd settle down and get married,' said Mam. They were eating their Sunday dinner, Mass behind them, an endless Sunday afternoon in front of them, no pubs open, the possibilities for entertainment few.

'Time enough,' said Brendan, opening out his floury potato and pushing butter into it.

'Aye,' said the old man. He was only looking at his food today, not even bothering to lift his knife and fork. 'Time enough. Wasn't I into my forties when I took the plunge.'

'And nearly out of them again,' said Mam.

'No need to rush into these things. Marry in haste and repent in leisure. Someone said that once. A man on his own is a . . . man . . . a man . . .' his voice became vague. 'A lucky man.'

134

'The thought hadn't even entered my mind, so you can both calm down. What's bitten you?'

He gave a murderous look in Joe's direction. Joe kept his eyes on his dinner.

'You're getting to the age now. There's lots of young fellas your age married with wains.'

'Fools, all fools. Fetch me over a bottle of stout from the shelf, Joe.'

Joe got up and fetched a bottle of stout. He put it and a glass down beside the untouched plate. His father put out a hand and touched the cool black bottle and belched.

'Ah, God. I feel better now.'

'Get a proper job and settle down.'

'Hasn't he got a job, woman? Wasn't he away all last week on a job?'

'A proper job. With a future. A bit of security. Money to buy a nice wee house with a bit of a garden. That's what I always wanted. I'd rather have stayed in the country, but I'd no choice. Back we had to come to the narrow streets of his lordship's childhood.'

'Hadn't I a right to live where I pleased? Isn't that any man's right? You never put up a complaint. In those days it was all lovey dovey and anything you want, me darling.'

'I had the idea you were going to work. Get out and earn a living, not just spend your life moaning to any fool that would listen.'

'Wasn't my health crippled?'

'Mauryah.'

He banged with the bottle on the table and all the plates rattled.

'No pity. No love.'

He roared like an animal that has been injured. Brendan leant over and took the bottle away from him. He continued to thump on the table with his fist. The gravy on his plate slopped over the edge and spread on the oilcloth.

'Pity,' she said with contempt. 'Why should anyone feel pity for you? You've never done a hand's turn in your life.

135

Sit up above like Lord Muck with your stout and your betting slips telling us all what a great hero you were. You say you're crippled. What about me? With you chained round my neck for life? Any pity I have in my heart is for myself and the fool I was. Would you give over that banging. You're not a child, and look at the good food all over the table.'

She got up and snatched away the plate from in front of him. She carried it out to the scullery and they could hear her scraping the food off it into the bucket. The old man leant back in his chair with his eyes shut, his breath catching in long sobs in the back of his throat. Brendan mashed the butter into his potato until it was all golden and shiny and then scooped up a forkful and put it into his mouth. Butter dribbled over his lips and down his chin. She came back into the room and sat down again.

'Pass me over the stout,' whispered the father.

'No,' she said. 'You've had enough.'

'Son . . .'

Brendan pushed the bottle across the table.

The man took the top off and tilted the bottle and the glass towards each other. Each one at the table watched the brown liquid creeping up the side of the glass, forming its collar of cream as it moved.

Please don't let anyone speak again, prayed Joe. Dear Father of Mercy, let no one utter, let us have only silence. The old man with the beard wasn't listening. Maybe he, also, was enjoying a quiet Sunday dinner.

'I knew.' Mam stared bitterly at Brendan.

'Where's the harm?'

'Respect. Even if not for me, for what I say.'

'I respect you all right.'

'You don't love me.'

'What's love? A word in too many mouths. Meaningless. Look around. Hate is a better word. I can understand that. You don't have to be long in this world to understand that word. We like to pretend it's not like that though, don't we?'

136

'Is that what you learnt in England?'

He ignored her. He turned to Joe.

'Write a poem about that, kiddo.'

He pushed his empty plate away.

'I'm off.'

He got up.

'Are you away without me again?'

'I am.'

'I . . .'

'There'll be other days, Dad.'

'I'm not well today.'

'Are you coming, Joe?'

'Me?'

'You.'

'Where are you taking the child?'

'There's some work he can do for me. Don't worry, Mam, I'll look after him all right. Coming Joe?'

Joe got quickly to his feet.

'Yeah.'

'I won't keep him late.'

'Do whatever suits you,' said his mother.

Brendan took Joe by the shoulder and pushed him out of the room.

'O.U.T.,' he muttered.

'Where are we going?' asked Joe once they were out in the street.

'I couldn't leave you there.'

'No.'

'I still have the car. She said she wouldn't come with me today unless I brought you too. That sounds as if I was mucking about. I wasn't. Just I think she likes you better than she likes me.'

Joe smiled.

'Anyway, I couldn't leave you there.'

'Where's the car?'

'At her place.'

'Mam hit me yesterday.'

137

'I expect you deserved it. She's nervous. Everyone's nervous. She doesn't want you to turn out like me.'

'How's that?'

'She doesn't trust me.'

'She wants you to go back to England.'

'She wants me to keep my nose clean, that's all. You'll do that for her, won't you, kiddo? You'll have the cleanest nose in the world.'

'I don't like you.'

'It's mutual.'

A brown Mini was parked outside the door of Kathleen's house. Brendan patted it like you might pat a dog. He felt in his pocket for the keys.

'You know, the old fellow's not as bad as she makes him out to be. He did his bit. You have to give him that.' He looked up towards Kathleen's window.

'Kathleen.'

The window above them rattled open.

'Hello, Joe.'

'Hello.'

'I'll be right down.'

'You have to give a man a chance. He's never really had a chance.'

Joe said nothing. There wasn't anything much to say.

They drove to a village on the western side of Lough Swilly. The sun was already starting on its westward slide as they drove up the side of the lough, and the shadows in the fields were long and slightly weird. A pair of swans on the muddy bank below a grey stone bridge plucked at their feathers with their strong beaks, their necks curved tenderly as they rummaged. Half a dozen cows cropped the rough grass in the ditch, unperturbed by the passing cars. Brendan drew up at the beginning of the village street, a long curling street by the water's edge.

'Look,' He pointed across the water towards a wide valley on the other side. 'Derry.'

138

Joe peered through the window.

'Where?'

'You can't see it, but it's there just the same. At night you can see the glow in the sky.'

He drove on. Two men sat on the sea wall smoking their pipes. They raised their hands in greeting as the car drove past. The windows of the houses stared at the sea. They had stared at the sea for several hundred years, they enjoyed their occupation. Brendan turned off the road on to a sandy slope by the pier. He parked the car beside a bus, which didn't look as if it intended to move for a long time.

'We'll walk.'

He opened the door for Kathleen to get out and offered her his hand. Joe scrambled out of the back. I won't be mean, he thought. I won't even think mean. I will smile. He smiled. Kathleen wrapped a scarf round her head and smiled. Brendan watched her face with care and slight anxiety. The beach was wide and gold. It curved out round a pile of rocks in the distance and disappeared. Beautiful old trees, now winter-grey, rose up a slight hill at the back of the beach and thickened into a wood. Along the water's edge a flock of leggy birds dipped their heads and pecked and moved and dipped again, like dancers. Brendan took Kathleen's arm and they walked, crunching their feet into the sand, towards the rocks. A man and his dog had walked that way before them and the sand was decorated with the prints of their feet.

'Kiu . . . kiu . . . kiu.'

A seagull lifted itself lazily from the water and flew a foot above the surface, its wings flapping almost impossibly slowly as it moved. Beyond the rocks, the beach stretched in a series of long curves, and the shadows of the trees stretched almost to the water's edge. On the other side of the lough the hills were blue and misty, but here they were brown and green with yellow hollows where the whins were already beginning to live again.

What is there for me, he wondered, if I can't make words

dance, as the birds are dancing? A man with a brush and tubes of colour can put these patterns on a page so that you can recognise them. Say, ah, yes. Can I, with a biro pen and a string of words? Where? How do you start? What are the rules? Do you just find them out as you go along? Trial and error. I don't want to drive the dry cleaner's van, or be an electrician. There should be someone you can talk to. One day my head will burst and words will spill out and be blown away by the wind and get caught in the branches of the trees. My words. Everybody's words, when you come to think about it, Oh, help. He looked at the two people walking ahead of him, their arms linked, his head bending slightly towards hers. Her long woollen skirt was blown backwards by the wind, her hair escaped from under the scarf. I found you, he thought with sadness.

As if he had called out to her, she turned at that moment, swinging Brendan with her, so that they both faced back towards the village once more.

'Let's go back.'

Their faces shone like polished apples.

'Come, Joe.'

She took his arm with her free hand.

'We'll have a cup of tea in the hotel. I saw a hotel. The sun will be gone soon and we might die of exposure.'

'I don't think I have enough money,' said Brendan. He put his hand into his pocket and began to count coins with his fingers.

'I have lots. I'll buy tea.'

'Oh, no . . .'

'Don't be silly, of course I will. You'd like tea, wouldn't you, Joe? She laced her fingers through his and pulled his hand into the pocket of her coat.

'Hot scones with runny butter and jam and . . . and . . . potato cakes.'

'Golly,' said Joe. 'I'd like that all right.'

'What a pair,' laughed Brendan.

The hotel was just across the road from the pier. Kathleen

kicked the sand off her shoes against a black metal foot scraper before going into the porch. An inside door led into a dark hall. Boop-a-dee-boop, a radio played somewhere. There was a smell of floor polish.

'I don't think they can be open.' The darkness made her whisper. 'There's a very closed feel about the place.'

A door opened and shut and a girl materialised out of the darkness and stood looking at them for a moment.

'Yes?'

'We wondered if we could have tea?' In spite of the fact that the girl had spoken in a normal voice, Brendan still whispered.

'Please,' said Kathleen, reprimanding him gently.

'Please.'

The girl must have been baking, the blue-checked apron round her waist was covered with flour. She rubbed at her fingers with a corner of it.

'There's a fire in the bar. I'll bring yeez tea in there. Just a pot mind. We don't do teas at this time of year.'

'That'd be great. Thanks.'

The girl waved a hand at a door on the right of the hall and disappeared down the passage again.

A good fire was burning in the bar, heaped high with spitting logs. Two men were standing against the bar with glasses of polished Guinness in front of them. They didn't bother to look round when the three strangers came in. They were discussing horse-racing in low voices, with the absorption of those whose lives might depend on the next word.

'A gorgeous fire.' Kathleen settled herself down beside it and held out her hands towards the heat. 'I like a wood fire. We always had wood at home. Snap, crackle and pop.' She laughed to herself.

'You're a queer one,' said Brendan, sitting down beside her.

'I bet we won't get scones and potato cakes here,' said Joe. He moved over towards the bar to try and pick up what the men were saying. It was nothing he could make head or tail of. A man came in to the back of the bar from a door leading into the hotel. He began mopping around with a cloth, as men behind bars always seem to be doing when they're not actually pouring drinks. He mopped away, his hand moving backwards and forwards and then round in circles, his head slightly bent towards the two men, his face mildly interested in what they were saying. By the fire, Kathleen and Brendan looked as if they had been sitting beside fires together for years. The girl they had spoken to in the hall bumped her way through the door, behind first, carrying a tray. She put it down on the table by the fire.

'There. It's only tea, but it'll warm yeez a bit.'

She stood and watched, as Kathleen leaned forward and picked up the stainless steel teapot.

'Are yeez from Derry?'

'That's right,' said Kathleen.

'I have a cousin works there in the hospital. Is it desperate?'

'You get used to it. Do you take sugar, Brendan?'

'Two.'

'Aye. That's what she says too. I don't think I'd fancy it at all. Sometimes we hear the explosions here.'

Her eyes were startled even by the recollection.

'It's the water,' explained Brendan. 'And the valley.'

She looked at him without comprehension.

Kathleen poured a cup of tea for Joe.

'Joe.'

'Thanks.'

He came over and sat down beside them.

'I thought I might go to Dublin.'

She still wiped her fingers on her apron. It seemed to be a nervous habit she had. Her fingers were quite clean. Brendan frowned into his cup of tea. Kathleen smiled at the girl.

'It's a great place.'

'I have a sister there. She works in Dunnes Stores. Do you know Dunnes Stores?'

'They're all over the place.'

'As like as not.'

Her finger would be polished to the bone soon, Joe thought.

'She'd like me to go up.'

'I'm sure she would.'

'I'd say Dublin would be a lot of crack.'

'You might be lonely.'

'Wouldn't I have my sister?'

'True.'

'Would the young fella like a biscuit?'

'Would you like a biscuit, Joe?' Kathleen winked at him, as she spoke.

'Yes, please.'

'I'll have a look and see what we've got.'

She walked slowly back across the bar, as if she had all the time in the world. She ignored the two men at the bar, and she ignored the barman, who had stopped mopping and was pulling two more glasses of stout.

'Isn't she a scream,' whispered Kathleen. 'Don't say a word.'

Brendan started to laugh.

'What are you laughing at?'

'You.'

'Me? Why me? What's so funny about me?'

He put out a hand and touched her knee.

'You're a scream, if anyone is.'

'Honestly.' She was a little put out by his words.

'Peeeeculiar,' said Joe. 'Very peeeculiar.'

'What's peculiar?' asked Brendan.

'She's peeeculiar. Imagine wanting to go and live in Dublin, when you could stay here.'

Brendan laughed abruptly.

'Kid talk.'

Joe shrugged.

'I hope it's chocolate biscuits.'

'You'll be lucky.'

He wasn't. It was rather soft digestive, crumbling slightly

round the edges, from either mice or extreme old age.

'Thank you,' he said to the girl, as she handed him the plate.

'That's O.K.'

After she had gone, he crumbled a couple of them in his fingers and dropped them into the fire.

They got back to the city about seven. Brendan pulled the car up outside Kathleen's house and sat in silence, his hands gripping the wheel.

'That was lovely, Brendan. Thank you,' said Kathleen gently. 'Would you like to come in for a while. You couldn't stay long, I have books to correct. You could have a cup of tea.'

'I must bring Joe home, thanks all the same.'

She pulled out the ashtray from the dashboard and killed her cigarette in it.

'Well.' She put out a hand to open the door.

'I have to be away all week again.'

A large drop of rain exploded on the windscreen.

'Rain,' said Joe.

'I should be back Friday.'

'Yes.'

There seemed to be no follow-up to the raindrop. Two army trucks roared past the end of the road.

'I'll pop round and see how you're situated.'

'Do that,' she said.

She opened the door. A very cold wind blew in. She got out quickly and banged the door. She thumped with her fist on the window.

'Bye.'

'Kathleen . . .'

'Bye, Joe.'

'See you.'

She ran up the steps. Brendan didn't drive off until she had turned the key in the door and she stood with one hand raised in farewell. The tall windows of the Cathedral were dimly lit as they drove past. Brendan drew the car over to the kerb and stopped.

'You go on home. I have to bring the car back. Tell Mam I won't be late home. I won't want any tea. I have to be away by half-eight in the morning. Tell her that.'

'Can't I come with you?'

'No. Get out.'

'Can I sleep in your bed when you're away?'

'Ask Mam.'

'She'll only say no.'

'Then, no.'

'It's my bed.'

Brendan leaned over and opened the door.

'Get out, can't you, and go home. You're wasting my time'.

Joe pushed the seat forward and clambered out.

'It's been a good day, hasn't it?' asked Brendan.

'Great.'

'Thanks for coming.'

Joe slammed the car door and walked home.

'Brendan's a nice boy.'

'He's O.K.'

They stood at their usual meeting place and looked over the rooftops at the walled city.

'What would Fred say?' he asked, with daring curiosity.

Smoke trickled out from between her lips as she stared across the valley.

'Whatever do you mean?' she asked eventually.

He blushed.

'Well, about you going out with Brendan? Won't he mind?'

'Silly Joe.'

That was all she said for a very long time.

He stood there beside her with his hands in his pockets and stared, like her, at the grey walls. The shouts of boys playing football drifted up from the playground below. After a long time, she repeated the words.

'Silly Joe.'

She dropped the last half-inch of her cigarette on the ground and stood on it.

'There's no harm in it . . . Fred would agree. No harm. I've been very lonely, Joe, and now, thanks to you, you first of all, and then Brendan, I'm not so lonely any more.' She put her hand on his shoulder. 'I have two friends, O.K.?'

'O.K.'

'It's a nice day.'

'Yes.'

'Have you time to come down and look at the boats?'

'Well . . .'

'Come on, quickly. I never go down to the quay, and I love boats.'

She shoved another cigarette into her mouth and, without lighting it, turned and went striding down the hill.

A building at the bottom of the hill was still smouldering and some workmen were clearing away the rubble. There was a queue at the army checkpoint and they stood there among the women with shopping baskets and prams, shuffling along a few feet at a time. Bags open. Shuffle. Kathleen lit her cigarette as they waited. Hands patting up and down you. 'Ta, love.' The faces remote as the hands slide over their bodies. 'Next.' Bags open. No love lost. 'Any bombs in the pram, love?' No time for jokes. Guns always at the ready. Bags open. Never turn your back on a Mick.

Feet shuffled and the shopping bags were moved from arm to arm, to ease the weight. The windows of the shops boarded and the Guildhall framed by scaffolding. Grey piles of stones and overhead the cannons pointing across the river. Their day was done.

A crane was working on the quay and they stood and watched it gently swing its load from ship to shore. A couple of men stood near them and watched also. Long lengths of timber were stacked on the wharf. Curled ropes and lengths of chain and the high buildings stained with flour dust. The cars moved slowly over the cobbles. Three men stood on the deck of a ship talking in low voices, their eyes warily on the movements of the crane. A cat sat near them, fluffing out its fur to keep the wind from penetrating.

'Look,' said Joe. 'A cat. They have a cat. Would you have thought of that?'

'A sea cat. Lots of boats have cats.'

'You wouldn't think they'd like the water.'

'I don't suppose they go near the water.'

'I mean storms and things. Suppose they get seasick?'

Kathleen laughed.

'Poor cat.'

They went closer to the edge of the wharf. The water slopped between the ship and the wall and an empty cigarette packet bobbed up and down. The cat got up and stretched itself, one leg at a time and then moved slowly in through a door, as if it owned the place. The men took their eyes off the crane for a moment and looked at Kathleen. Seagulls wheeled and mewed. The wind made the flags dance. One of the men shouted something at Kathleen in a foreign language. She smiled and waved at him. He had very white teeth, like china cups, Joe thought. Water foamed suddenly out of a hole in the side of the ship.

'Someone is pulling the chain,' he said.

'Or washing up,' suggested Kathleen.

'Or having a bath.'

'Or brushing their teeth.'

Joe saw a whole row of men brushing their white china teeth and spitting, simultaneously, peppermint-flavoured foam into a big hole.

'That's what they're doing,' he said.

They walked on down the quay, stepping with care over the ropes and chains and watching the water change in colour as the sun went behind the hill. There was only the one ship moored and the whole place had a lonely and rather melancholy feeling about it.

'Home, James,' she said suddenly.

'Who's James?'

'I don't know. It's just something my father used to say. Home, James, and don't spare the horses. It comes into my mind from time to time. It has a sort of ring about it.'

They turned up a narrow street away from the water. From far away down the river came the twitter of the six o'clock hooter from the power station.

'I'll be massacred.'

He started to run, leaving her behind. After a few yards he remembered her and turned.

'I must fly.'

'Goodbye, sparrow.'

The lights on the lamp standards looked like diamonds in the pale evening light.

There was no row when he got home. His mother was sitting at the table reading the *Journal*. The sound of the radio in his father's room was muted. She looked up at him as he came in, his mouth and throat full of apologies and lies. 'The evenings are drawing out now.' She said nothing else, looked back down at the photographs of smiling brides, who didn't know what they were letting themselves in for.

'I'll have your tea for you in a few minutes. Go and wash your hands.'

Out in the scullery he held his hands under the tap and watched the water bouncing off them into the sink.

A cat strolls,
Black with green eyes,
On the wet deck,
Hoping
Against hope
That he won't fall into the sea.

He laughed out aloud.

'What's so funny?' Her voice called to him from the kitchen.

'Nothing.'

His hands were red after the cold water. He dried them carefully on the roller towel.

'Share the joke.'

'It was only something inside my head made me laugh.'

He sat down at his place. She had folded the paper away and was getting the plates out of the oven.

'Is Dad not coming down?'

'He's suffering.'

'Is he bad?'

'He's dead, but he won't lie down.'

Fried black pudding and tomatoes. Chips.

'Ooh, chips.'

She leaned across the table and poured his tea.

'Did you ever see a cat on a boat?'

'Eat your tea before it gets cold and don't be asking silly questions.'

It was a couple of days after that two more soldiers were shot dead. Joe and Peter were just coming out of school when the patrol went past them. Three of the men were walking forwards and the fourth backwards, his head moving from side to side, his hands gripping tight on to his gun. The boys barely noticed them. Joe had one eye out for Kathleen as they went down the hill, but there was no sign of her.

'What'll we do?' asked Peter.

'I don't mind.'

'Football?'

'I don't mind.'

'You're all go these days. What's up with you?'

'Nothing. Football would be great.'

'If that's what you'd like.'

'Yeah.'

The two shots were loud and very close. The sound of them echoed down the street for a moment and then there was total silence. A few birds flew up in the air and hovered before settling down again.

149

Peter seemed to be the first person in the whole city to break the silence. 'Wow.'

'Armalite,' said Joe.

'Yes.'

They stood where they were, uncertain what to do. The street seemed very empty. There was the sound of some orders being shouted from round the corner and then some rapid shooting.

'What do you think's up?'

Joe shook his head.

'Will we go and have a look?'

'No.'

'No.'

A figure turned into the road along at the corner. It was Kathleen. She began to run towards them. Two army trucks hurtled over the crossroads. He moved slowly towards Kathleen

'Don't go up there.' Her face was white. She gripped his shoulder fiercely with her fingers. 'Don't go.'

'What happened?'

'They shot two soldiers . . . just there . . . just . . . don't go.'

'I'm not going.'

'Don't go.' It seemed all she could say. Tears slid down her cheeks.

'I'll just run up and have a quick gawk,' said Peter.

'Don't,' she said.

Peter moved away from them towards the corner. Joe put his arm around her.

'It's all right. I won't go.'

She pushed at the tears with her hand.

'I was there. Right beside them. Just walking . . . just . . .'

'Have a cigarette.'

'It was just past the corner. One of them fell into the road. I thought, oh God, he'll be run over if a car comes round the corner. Wasn't that a silly thing to think?'

'Well, he might have been.'

'It wouldn't have mattered. He got it right in the middle of the head.'

She rubbed fiercely at her face with her hand. Another truck went past them. Peter stood up by the corner, not moving. An ambulance siren was whining towards them.

'I've never seen . . .'

'Come back home with me and have a cup of tea.'

Mam would have a fit, but there was nothing else he could say.

She shook her head.

'I've never . . . no . . . I'll go home. Promise. Don't muck about. Just go home.'

'I'll walk up with you.'

'No. Just go home. You wouldn't know what sort of trouble there might be . . .'

She felt at her face with her fingers, feeling the reality of it, the livingness of it.

An ambulance screamed across the road.

'Come on. Come, Joe.'

They crossed the road and walked slowly towards the corner. Peter still stood by the corner motionless. Not even a curtain twitched. No one breathed. The tobacconist on the corner was locking his door as they went past. He nodded briefly at them, but said nothing.

'Run away on home now, Joe. Quick. Maybe I'll see you tomorrow.'

He ran until he reached the house. His father began thumping on the floor as soon as he heard him in the hall. Joe dropped his school bag on the floor and went up to him.

'What is it?'

'I want my tea.'

He was like some evil old demon propped up there in his grey pyjamas with an old jersey pulled over the top of them. His eyes were a dirty grey like the pyjamas.

'Give me time to take my coat off, can't you?'

'My tongue is hanging out.'

'I'll get it for you in a minute.'

'And then you can run up the road and get me a couple of bottles of stout. Before she comes in.'

'There's shooting.'

'Ah.' He leaned back against the crumpled pillows. 'I thought I heard something.'

'Two soldiers.'

'Dead?'

'I don't know. Hit anyway. Dead, I think.'

They could hear the ambulances in the distance.

The old man smiled.

'That's as good as a tonic. Go you on down and get the tea. I'll be down after you.'

Joe rattled the fire and filled it, listening all the time to the heavy movements from the man in the room above. He put the kettle on and wondered what a man would look like that had had a hole blown in his head. There was a bang on the door. He went and opened it. Peter stood there.

'She told me to come on home,' said Joe. 'So I did. I'm sorry.'

'I'm on my way home too.'

'Do you want to come in?'

Peter shook his head. They stood looking at each other.

'Did you see anything.'

'They covered them up with red blankets.'

'Does that mean . . .?'

'I'd better get on. They have to wash the street. Did you know that?'

'Red blankets?'

'It's always red blankets. I'd better get on.'

'See you.'

'See you.'

'Who's that at the door, Joe?' His father was on the stairs.

Peter ran down the hill. Joe closed the door and went back into the kitchen.

'Did you not hear me? Who was it?' He was nearly half-way down.

'Peter.'
'Who's Peter when he's at home?'
'My friend.'
He heard his mother at the door.
'Are you in, Joe?'
She closed the door and came along the passage.
'I'm in.'
She came into the kitchen.
'I'm glad of that.'
She became aware of the old man.
'So you're getting up.'
'Have you heard the news?'
'I suppose you're away off to celebrate.'
'Cause for celebration.'
Joe put the teapot on the table.
'I've made the tea.'
'Thanks, son.'
Dad reached the bottom of the stairs, clutching on to the banister rail. He threw his head back in a dramatic gesture and began to sing.
'A nation once again . . .'
'If you want a cup of tea, sit down in peace and have it.'
'A nation once again . . .'
'Did you hear me?'
'Two of the enemy are dead.'
'Two children.'
'What do you mean, children?'
'That's all they were. Younger than Brendan.'
'Enemy soldiers. What sort of a traitor do you think you are to moan over enemy soldiers?'
'I'm no traitor and you know it. Sit down and take your tea and get a hold of your wits, if you have any.' She laughed as he moved slowly across the room to his chair. 'If you ever had any.' She sat down herself at the table and Joe pushed a cup of tea over to her. She held her hands out in front of her and looked at them. She opened them and shut them, moved her fingers stiffly. Her fingers absorbed her,

the swollen joints, the scraped look of the skin, the white flecks on her ridged nails.

The old man began to sing again.

'A nation once again . . .' An ancient, destroyed voice.

She dragged her eyes away from her hands and looked up at him.

'It's old buggers like you should be shot, with your talk and your singing of glory and heroes.'

'Freedom . . .'

'What's freedom?'

'Don't be a fool, woman. You know well what freedom is. Didn't I fight for freedom? Didn't I give my health? What did Pearse, God rest him, say about freedom?'

'Well, you don't remember, that's for sure. Have they any more freedom down there than we have up here?'

'You misunderstand . . .'

'Is there a job for every man? And a home for everyone? Have all the children got shoes on their feet? Are there women down there scrubbing floors to keep the home together because stupid, useless old men are sitting round gassing about freedom? Singing their songs about heroes?' Her voice had risen almost to a scream. He looked at her in silence for a very long time. Then he started to move towards the door, crippled with pain. The pain she had inflicted on him. The pain of the world of forgotten heroes. At the door he turned. 'You are disgusting. Disgusting.'

'Did they even give you a pension?'

'I talk about freedom. You talk about shoes and pensions.'

'Take your bloody fairy tales out of this house before I . . .' She began to cry hopelessly. That's two people have cried today, thought Joe. I wonder how many more.

His father shuffled down the passage and pulled his muffler off the hook by the door.

'Before what?' He taunted her. 'I'll get out of my own house in my own good time and no befores or beafters from you.'

She rubbed at her face.

154

'Ah, go,' was all she said.

They heard the hall door open and then close and the shuffling of his feet on the path. She clasped her two hands round her cup of tea.

'God forgive me,' she prayed. 'For the thoughts in my head.'

'Drink your tea, Mam.'

He was frightened by tears. Not by children's tears of rage or pain, nor his father's blubberings of self-pity, but adult tears like hers and Kathleen's which made him feel that the world might crack open suddenly.

'I'll go up and do my homework.'

'Aye son. Do that.'

He picked up his school bag and left her sitting at the table with the three untasted cups of tea.

After a while she called him to come down and they ate their tea in silence. Her eyelids were red and ugly. A bomb went off over in the direction of the city. The china on the table clattered for a moment and the bulb above them trembled at the end of the flex. Still she didn't speak. Her mouth tightened and she glanced quickly across the table at him. That was all.

'Bring your books down here. It's cold in your room,' she said, when he had finished eating.

He found it hard to concentrate with her in the mood she was in. Normally she would be busy around the place, or balanced, rather than sitting, on her chair, bent over the mending, her hand groping out over the table from time to time for her scissors or the thread. Now she sat, staring at nothing, her hands lying exhausted in her lap. He tried, unsuccessfully, for a long time and then laid his pen down on the table in front of him.

'It's not Brendan you know, Mam. That's what you're thinking, isn't it?'

'What do you know about it, or what I'm thinking? Get on with your studies.'

He turned to the middle page of his exercise book and

wrote out the poem about the cat. He looked at the words for a long time, aware constantly of his mother's gauntness across the table. A poem must have substance. Kathleen had said that to him once. Be more than a word picture. How can words have substance? That was something you could hold in your hand. His fingers clenched on his substantial pen. He thought of the cat, unblinking on the deck, and its stretching legs, claws pricking for a moment into the wood of the deck, its sleek sides plumped out with food and confidence.

His mother sighed.

He drew two lines diagonally across the words, crossing each other in the middle like the lines on a flag. The insubstantial cat existed no longer. He would have to remember to pull out that page before he got to school. He shut the book and reached for his school bag. He gathered up the books on the table and packed them neatly into it. He fastened the frayed straps.

'Are you through, son?'

Her voice startled him. He had almost forgotten that she could speak.

'Yes.'

'There's no sign of your Daddy.'

'No.'

'He must have found someone to have a drink with.'

'Yes.'

'He'd have been home otherwise.'

'Yes.'

'Leave off your shoes and I'll clean them for the morning.'

He took them off and left them on the chair. The lino was cold through his socks.

'Night, Mam.'

'Night, son.'

She didn't move from her seat.

He kept his socks on in bed. She wouldn't have liked that if she'd known, but he had always found that if he got into bed with cold feet, he usually woke up in the morning with

156

cold feet. He didn't sleep through till morning though, as the army came in at each end of the street at about two o'clock and began a house-to-house search. He heard the disturbance in his sleep first, a confused dream of shouts and bangs and running feet. It was the sudden sound of breaking glass that made him open his eyes. He got out of his bed and climbed on to Brendan's to peer out through the small window. Half the people in the street seemed to be outside, standing in silence, watching the organised destruction. He shifted his legs so that he could lean forward to see whose house they had reached. His knee banged against something hard under the covers. He groped under the clothes with his hand and his fingers found something even colder than his feet. He got off the bed and pulled back the clothes. A gun lay on the crumpled sheet. He looked at it unhappily. He didn't know anything about guns, but there was no doubt about what it was. No toy. Black and cool. No plastic bang-bang toy.

They were hammering on Mrs O'Toole's door now. They wouldn't be there too long. One old lady and her hens can't be too much of a menace. He hoped they wouldn't worry the hens too much or they might go off laying and she depended on the eggs. The gun was still there. He heard his mother moving in her room. Dressing. She wouldn't like to be turned out into the street in her nightie. His heart was leaping in his chest and throat. He watched his hand creep out very slowly and his fingers hover for a moment before touching it again. Cold. What a stupid place to leave a gun. He could hear them running up Mrs O'Toole's stairs and banging open the cupboards in her room. He picked up the gun. There was nothing else to do. It was surprisingly heavy. He wondered was it loaded. Oh, God. His father was snoring. He must have had a lot of drink taken. He looked around the room. Oh, God. His mother put curlers in her hair every night. He wondered if she would take them out or cover her head with her blue woollen scarf. Please God. His school bag was lying on the floor by his bed.

'Joe.'

'Yes, Mam.' He whispered the words.

'Are you awake, Joe?'

It was the sound of more glass breaking that made him move.

'I'll be right down Mam.'

'I can't wake your Daddy.'

He opened the straps of the school bag and pushed the gun down among his books. Meisse agus Pangur Bán and the equilateral triangle. He pushed it well down to the bottom. He adjusted his English grammar. You couldn't see it if you only looked. He fastened the straps again and slung the bag over his shoulder. 'Joe, are you deaf?'

He remembered the bed.

'Coming.'

He pulled the bedclothes up and patted at them. It didn't look too bad. He opened the door. His mother was standing there. There was a sudden wild cackling from the yard next door.

Oh, chooks.

'He's out cold,' she said. 'I'll just have to leave him.' It was their turn. The house shook with the hammering on the door.

'Coming.' Her voice was shrill. She ran down the stairs. She had the blue scarf tied round her head. She opened the door. Joe was just behind her, clutching at the school bag.

Four soldiers crowded into the passage.

'Outside. Come on, all out.'

'Put on your coat, Joe.'

'Get a move on, missus.'

'My husband . . .'

'What about your husband? Ey? Locked up in jail, is he?'

'No. He's . . .'

'Out, and the kid.'

'He's sick . . . in bed . . .'

He gave her a shove out into the dark and pushed Joe after her. Once he was out of the house he felt sick. They joined the silent crowd. Old Mrs O'Toole was crying quietly. Joe's mother went and stood beside her. The people's faces were tired and angry. A soldier came out of Mrs O'Toole's house with a couple of eggs in his hand. He showed them to a friend.

'A couple of hand grenades for breakfast.' He laughed and put them carefully into his two breast pockets.

'Bastards,' shouted a woman's voice from down the street.

'Shut up, love,' said one of the soldiers calmly. 'Or we'll shoot the lot of you.'

Several children were crying.

A soldier appeared at the door and called Joe's mother over.

'Here, you.'

'Me?'

'Yeah, you. What's up with the old man?'

'I told you. He's ill.'

'Drunk, more like.'

'He's maybe drunk, but he's ill with it. He's been ill for years.'

'We'll have to move him.'

'Well, move him,' she said with sudden anger.

'He's not likely to die on us or anything?'

'That's your problem.'

She moved back to Mrs O'Toole. The old woman's hair hung down over her shoulders in wispy grey plaits. She had a blanket thrown round her shoulders. She looked cold and very unsure of what was going on.

'I never done anything,' she said to Joe's mother. 'I never . . .'

'Sure,' Mam's voice was ironical, 'we're all as innocent as new-born babes.'

The soldier who had taken the eggs came up to them.

'You can go back in now, granny. We've finished with you.'

'Can I go in with her and settle her? I'm sure you have the place ruined on her. She's old.'

He looked Mam up and down.

'I suppose so. No hanky-panky though or you'll be in trouble.' He gave an almost human smile, 'and so will I.'

'Hanky panky,' said Mam with scorn.

She took the old woman's arm and they both went into the house.

If you gave that fellow a good push in the chest, thought Joe, those eggs would break. That'd be a laugh . . . or maybe it wouldn't. His feet were frozen. He clutched the school bag close to his side and did a little dance for warmth. He wondered what they would do with Dad. Turf him out onto the floor, as like as not. He had to smile at the thought.

After about half an hour they were allowed back into the house. The cupboards had been pulled out from the walls and most of the drawers emptied on to the floor. They had raked out the fire from inside the stove. Even the dustbin in the yard had been turned over and the week's rubbish was blowing round trying to escape. They had gone through the anthracite and left black boot-marks all over the kitchen floor. Mam had two geranium plants that she nursed carefully on the window sill in the front room, now the plants lay on the floor, the earth scattered round them. She picked them up and stood with one plant in each hand. The head of one of them was broken.

'Go on up to your bed,' she said to Joe. 'I'll straighten the place in the morning.'

'I could give you a hand.'

He still had the school bag tight under his arm.

'No, son. You won't be fit for school if you don't get some sleep. I'm all right. My plants.'

She bent down and began to scoop the earth off the floor and press it back into the pots.

'My plants.'

'I'm cold,' said Joe.

'Weren't you the fool to go out without your shoes. You'll warm up in bed. Look in on your Daddy on the way past.'

'I could help.'

'Just do what you're told.' Her voice was tired to death. Her fingers pressed and soothed the dry earth, pushed the roots in firmly, nipped off the broken head. She was crying very quietly again. He just did what he was told. His father was sitting in a chair in the middle of the room. Around him on the floor were tossed the sheets and blankets from the bed. He was dressed in his shirt and trousers. He had probably got into bed like that when he had come in. He stared at Joe as if he had never seen him before. He was still very drunk.

'I said to them, get out, you bloody British bastards.'

Newspapers and dirty clothes were heaped on the floor with the blankets. There was a pile of soot on the floor beside the fireplace. The doors of the press were hanging open.

He pulled himself together suddenly.

'Is it, Joe?'

'Aye.'

'Where's your Mammy?'

'Below.'

'Tell her to come up and make my bed for me.'

'I'll do it.'

'Your Mammy.'

'She's busy. They left a terrible mess.'

'I said to them . . .'

'You told me what you said to them.'

The sheets were grey and smelled of illness. He tucked them on to the bed and then the blankets. He shook the pillows and a couple of feathers drifted down on to the floor. The old man sat all the while muttering to himself and coughing.

'I said to them . . .'

'Come on. Get in.'

'You'll have to give me a hand. I've stiffened up with the cold.'

He hated to touch the old man. He was always afraid that

161

his fingers would sink through the soft, mouldering skin.

'Substance.' He said it for courage and put a hand under his father's elbow.

'What's that?'

'Nothing.'

'Bloody British murderers, get out of this country, I said.'

'You're lucky they didn't take you away with them.'

He heaved and the old man came up on to his feet.

'That's what I said anyway. They could have shot me and I wouldn't have cared.'

Neither would I, only the mess would have been terrible.

They moved slowly to the bed and he pushed his father down on to it.

'There.'

'I'm cold.'

'So am I. Mam and I were out in the street for ages.'

'That's what I said to them. They didn't like it, I can tell you that.'

He fell back against the pillows and began to cough. Joe covered him with the bedclothes and picking up the school bag left the room. He closed the door behind him.

'Is he all right?' she called up to him.

'He's all right.'

He pictured her still standing there with the flower pot in her hand, the crumpled skin of her face grey. It wasn't love he felt when he thought of her, only a kind of exasperated pity.

He waded through the mess on his bedroom floor and sat down on Brendan's bed, his bed. He put the bag down beside him. He was too tired to think about anything. Tomorrow, he thought as he bent down and picked up a pillow from the floor and a couple of blankets. Tomorrow. He wrapped the blankets round himself and the school bag. He didn't care what anyone said about which bed he slept in. Tomorrow. He fell asleep.

She had to wake him. Shaking at his shoulder, pulling and plucking at his pyjamas. Suddenly his eyes were open and he was looking at her. She looked as if she hadn't been to bed at all.

'You're nearly late. Get up. I thought you'd never wake.'

She kept a grip on his shoulder as if to prevent him from falling back into sleep again.

'Yes.'

'What in the name of God have you your schoolbag in there for?'

'I didn't want to forget it,' he said stupidly. He remembered what was in it. His head began to worry. She gave a final shake at his shoulder.

'Your breakfast's waiting.'

'I'll be down.'

It was cold outside the blankets and he had to search through all the mess on the floor for his clothes. She had done a lot of clearing downstairs and the kitchen looked the same as usual. The stove was lighting and porridge steamed on the table.

'Eat up quickly now, you've not much time.'

'You've tidied up.'

'Someone had to.'

He had the bag on his knee, crushed between his chest and the table. He wondered what they would do to him if they found the gun tucked in under his English grammar. The great thing was to get rid of it quickly. After school. It'd be all right in school. Afterwards though. The heat of the porridge slipping down his throat made him feel a bit better.

The street was littered with debris from the night before. People picked their way with distaste and resignation through the mess. In every house Joe knew that women were shaking out the clothes and packing them back into drawers again, brushing out the corners now exposed, where cupboards had hidden the dust, repairing damage. Sick of it all. They had been lucky. Sometimes floorboards were ripped up and pictures thrown from the walls. Men were lifted, and young fellas too. Mam had that to be thankful for.

During break-time he stood by the wall in the playground, the bag under his right arm.

'I have toothache,' he said, when they called him to come and play.

'What's up?'

Peter slid up beside him.

'I have a toothache.'

'Bad?'

'Aye. Bad enough.'

'Hard luck. Hard cheese. Come and play. Take your mind off it.'

Joe shook his head.

'Right.'

Peter was off. Joe felt the beginning of an ache creep along his bottom jaw and stretch up towards his right ear. Oh, damn. Oh, odd. It would be the last straw to have a toothache, as well as a gun in your school bag. No toothache, please, God. Oh, Queen of Heaven, overlook my white lie. My toothpaste lie. You must realise the situation. This is no time for truth. He felt she might be more sympathetic towards his problem than the Almighty himself. Oh, Blessed Mother, forgive me all my sins, my lies. I'll never, ever, sin again if you get me through this. Try never to sin, he corrected himself. No point in sticking your neck out.

'How is it?'

'What?'

He was startled by Peter's reappearance.

'The tooth.'

'Oh . . . awful. Awful.' He rubbed his jaw.

'Maybe you'll have to have it out.'

'Maybe I will.'

'Scrrruuunch.'

Peter performed a cork-pulling operation with his hands.

'Fuck off, can't you.'

'Oooh, bad. What would your Mammy say?'

'You heard.'

He balled his fist. His free fist.

'Temper.'

Peter moved away.

'Perhaps he'll pull them all out.'

Rain had set in by the time that school was over. That was a good thing really as it meant that most people set off quickly for home and there wasn't too much mucking around.

He pulled the hood of his anorak up over his head and ran. The rain made a good excuse for running. He didn't want to be the only running person in the whole city. He ran as fast as he could, not looking to left or right in case he saw Kathleen. There was nobody much about. A few wet prams stood outside the shops under the flats. The windows of the shops themselves were steamed over. Some gardeners from the council stamped their feet with cold and impatience as they waited in the shelter of the flats for the rain to slacken off. Their spades and forks grew like plants from the newly-turned earth on the hillside. The high grey walls had seen it all before. Tragedy, comedy, guns in small boys' school bags, left them cold. He walked soberly up the steps. His trousers were all splashed with mud. His jaw throbbed dismally. There was no one else at the checkpoint. The soldiers were laughing at some joke.

'You're a bit wet, aren't you, son?' said one of them to Joe.

He nodded and smiled, a wide disarming smile. He tried hard to keep the smile in position as he opened the school bag and held it out towards the soldier. The man barely glanced into it.

'That's O.K.' He ran his hands briefly over Joe's body and gave him a friendly shove on the shoulder.

'Tara.'

Safe. He walked quickly across the road. Almost safe. Almost. He went down a narrow street and on to the quay.

Cars moved slowly, nose to tail. The cranes were motionless.
A couple of dockers talked and smoked in the shelter of one
of the warehouses. The seagulls on the rooftops were
hunched down into themselves, like sick old men. He walked
slowly along the edge of the wharf. In front of him a timber
ship lay, its flags sad in the rain. He stepped carefully over
one of the huge ropes attaching it to the wharf. He opened
his bag and groped into it with cold, wet fingers. A man in
a blue jersey leaned over the ship's rail smoking. He didn't
seem to mind the rain. He dropped his butt in the river and
turned away. Joe pulled the gun out of the bag and dropped
it down the side of the wharf. It seemed to fall so slowly.
Slower than anything before had ever fallen. He stood,
rooted to the ground, waiting for it to disappear, be gone.
It splashed into the water, and mesmerising circles grew out
and out towards the centre of the river. He dropped the bag
on the ground and, leaning out over the brown water, was
sick. A white gush of water poured out from the side of the
ship. There was turbulence. There was definitely no longer
any gun.

'Hey, hey, you boy.'

The man in the blue jersey called down to him.

'You O.K.?'

'I've been sick.'

'You eat too much dinner?'

'Yeah.'

He wiped at his mouth with the sleeve of his anorak. He
turned away from the water abruptly.

'You O.K. Boy? Hey?' The voice was deep and foreign,
kindly though, really kindly.

Joe nodded up at him.

'I'm fine, thanks. I'll just . . .'

There was a long pause. The man reached into his pocket
for another cigarette.

'You go home now to your Mama. Yes.'

He waved cheerfully. Joe waved back.

'Bye.'

Lights from the shop windows made patterns on the wet roads. He wondered where Brendan was. Somewhere, driving his lorry through the rain, the wipers rhythmically pushing the rain across the windscreen. Would he have heard the news? Homes raided. House-to-house search. A quantity of arms and ammunition . . . damn, damn silly of him to leave a gun lying around in a place like that. Careless. His school bag felt joyfully light. His toothache had definitely gone.

He wondered how many other guns were down there at the bottom of the river. Hundreds of years of guns, slowly being eaten away with the action of the water.

He heard Mam moving in the kitchen as he hung his wet anorak on the hook.

'Is that you, Joe?'

'Yes.'

She appeared in the kitchen door. Her face was too tired even to show anger.

'How many times do I have to tell you to come straight home? Where were you?'

'I walked part of the way with Peter.' Here we go again.

'In this weather. Look at your trousers. You're soaked through. When will you learn a bit of sense? Away up and change your trousers before you get pneumonia.'

'I'm all right.'

She raised her hand and moved towards him. It was more than he could bear. He began to cry. She stopped.

'Son . . . son.' She turned and went back into the kitchen. 'Change your trousers,' she called back over her shoulder.

He went upstairs. There was no sound from his father's room. Mam had the whole place to rights. His bed and Brendan's neatly made and the clothes back in the press. She was filling the kettle. He heard the sound of the water knocking in the pipe. A good sound. He sat on the edge of the bed that should have been his bed. He knew his wet trousers were making a dirty mark on the cover, but he didn't care. He thought about his secret. His heroic secret. He smiled at that thought. He and the river . . . oh, and what about the man in the blue jersey? No. He was just a nice man. Concerned. Only he and the river and the flags that hung over the hull. Now there was a word . . . a good word. Perhaps it would be a good thing to be a sailor in a blue jersey. Inside the hull there would be a warm core. It would be just his luck to get seasick.

'You O.K., boy?'

'I'm fine.'

'Come aboard the hull, boy. You'd make a good sailor. I can see it in your face.'

'Joe.'

Hulls and sea gulls, pecking, burrowing away with their beaks, deep under their wings. Mean-eyed gulls.

'Joe.'

He wiped the tears off his face with the sleeve of his jersey.

'How many times do I have to call you? Your tea's waiting.'

He got up and went across the room.

'Coming.'

She was standing at the bottom of the stairs.

'What didn't you change your trousers?'

'I forgot.'

'God, give me patience.'

'I'm sorry. I'll do it now.'

He went back into the room again.

'Be quick.'

He was quick. He let no thoughts come between himself and his dry trousers.

'Pneumonia you'll get,' was all she said when he went down again.

Shepherds pie.

'You have the whole place looking great.'

'I've cleaned up.'

'Where's Dada?'

'Your guess is as good as mine.'

She took a long suck of tea and held it in her mouth,

savouring its sweetness, before swallowing it.

'When he realised I wasn't going to work, he was up and dressed and away out. Limping and spitting.'

'You didn't go to work?'

'No.'

'Will they mind?'

'They wouldn't need to. I've never let them down before.'

The wind threw a handful of rain against the window. She looked round, with sudden fright.

'It's only rain,' he said.

'My nerves are getting bad again.'

'The rain's been bad all day. Is Brendan home yet?' He asked the question casually.

'No.'

'Oh.'

He was beginning to feel warm and comfortable.

'This is nice.'

'I'm glad you like it, son.'

She smiled at him. Suddenly it was quite like old times again, before Brendan had come back.

'Can I have some more?'

'I'd better keep some for Brendan.'

He banged his knife and fork down on his plate.

'There's plenty of bread.'

'Maybe he won't come home.'

'Of course he'll come home. What makes you say a silly thing like that?'

I know something you don't know about precious Brendan.

'He might be meeting his friends.'

'He might, but you're not eating his supper just the same.'

'Nothing,' he said, with dignity, 'was further from my mind.'

'Some jam?' She pushed the pot towards him, appeasingly.

The door opened.

'Brendan?'

'I'll have jam,' said Joe.

169

'I'll be right down.'

Joe listened to his feet on the stairs and the sound of him moving round the room above. He buttered a slice of bread and then spread it with jam. It was the thick, gluey strawberry jam again. Why could she never buy anything else for a change?

'Cut it,' said his mother. 'Cut it. Don't be eating like a savage.'

The steps came slowly down the stairs. Brendan came into the kitchen.

'I have your tea waiting . . .'

'Were they here?'

His mother got up and went over to the oven, Joe cut the bread in half and stuck the two pieces together to make a sandwich.

'Who?' asked Mam.

'You know well who. The soldiers. Have they been here?'

She put his plate on the table.

'Of course they've been here. They've been everywhere. Sit down and take your tea.'

'I don't want any tea.'

The glue sandwich could have been worse. He stared at Brendan as he chewed, passing information with his eyes. They said you could do it. Concentration was what they said you needed. They were wrong.

'I cooked it for you.'

'I'm sorry, Mam.' He didn't move.

She shrugged.

'What did they do?' His eyes wandered round the room, searching for signs of violation.

'What do you think they did? They turned the place up-side down, so they did. I spent all night and all day cleaning up after them. And Mrs O'Toole's place. She's old. She was upset. I had to give her a hand.'

'Bastards.'

'They're no worse than the next man. They only do what they do because of people like you and your father. You and your . . .' she searched for a word '. . . tripe. Tripe.'

He ignored her. 'Did they find much?'

'A good bit, they say, and three lads lifted.'

'Did they . . .? What are you gawping at me like that for?'

Joe shook his head.

'I'm not gawping.' So much for concentration and thought waves.

'Gawping is what I'd call it.'

Joe took another piece of bread and went through the glueing process again.

'Is Dad above?'

'I don't know where your father is. If you're not going to eat your food, I'll give it to the child.'

'I don't want it,' said Joe.

'You wanted it ten minutes ago.'

'Well, I don't want it now.'

She looked exasperated.

'You cleaned up everything?'

'Of course I did. Who else did you think did it?'

She sat down and poured herself a cup of tea.

'Were they upstairs?'

'They were upstairs and downstairs and in my lady's chamber. They were in the dustbins and Mrs O'Toole's hens.'

'They threw the beds all over the floor,' said Joe with malice.

'Would you not eat a couple of mouthfuls?'

'For God's sake . . . all women want to do is stuff you full of food. I've eaten if it makes you feel better.'

'Oh.' She didn't believe him.

Joe licked the jam from round the edges of his mouth. He pushed his chair back from the table and stood up.

'Where are you off to?'

'To get my books. I left them upstairs.'

He turned his back on his mother and walked towards the door. He stared straight into his brother's face. Damn you, thicko, damn you, understand.

'You've obviously gone demented,' was all his brother said, as he moved to let Joe past.

'Don't be always at him.'

At the top of the stairs he called down to his brother.

'Brendan.'

Brendan put his head out of the door and looked up at him.

'What is it?'

Joe made a gun with his fingers and thumb and pointed it at his brother.

'Up.'

Brendan ran up the stairs. He pushed Joe into the room and shut the door.

'Well?'

He took Joe's wrist and squeezed it.

'You're hurting me.'

'Well?' He relaxed his grip a little.

'It's all right. I dealt with the whole thing.' Heroics. The fingers tightened on his wrist.

'You mean they didn't get it?'

Joe shook his head.

'Ow.'

'Well?'

'I took it. I hid it.'

Brendan let go of his wrist.

'Good man. Great. God, I was worried. I nearly didn't come home in case they were waiting for me.'

He patted Joe's shoulder.

'Good lad.'

They stood looking at each other.

'Well? Where is it?'

He whispered the words. Below in the kitchen they could hear her putting away the tea things.

'I got rid of it,' said Joe with pride. 'It's gone.'

'Right. Great. But where?'

'I threw it in the river.'

'You're having me on.'

172

'No. Why would I do that? I had to do something with it. I couldn't have kept it . . . Honestly.' He looked at Brendan with alarm. 'I couldn't have kept it . . . I threw it in the river. Well . . . dropped . . . sort of slithered it in. No one saw me.' Heroic.

Brendan looked at him in silence for a long time and then gently squeezed his shoulder.

'That's O.K., kiddo. Thanks.'

He opened the door and started down the stairs.

'What should I have done? Can you tell me that?'

'You were great.'

'Honest?'

'Honest.'

Brendan put his head into the kitchen.

'I'll be back, Mam.'

He flicked a hand in Joe's direction and went out of the house, closing the door quietly behind him.

Joe's father came in about an hour after Joe had gone to bed. He could hear the discords of their voices through the floor. One day he could just go, and never hear the voices any more. Step out the door as Brendan had, but never come back, as Brendan had. Never. Always in this city he would hear their voices, feel their pain. Perhaps it would be the same wherever he went. Perhaps you could never escape.

His father's feet stumbled up the stairs and his door slammed. The mumbling of his voice came through the wall, and the coughing. Eternal coughing. Outside, the wind was blowing a hardboard sheet against a window-frame and the rain splashed ceaselessly.

'Hello,' he whispered, when Brendan eventually came in.

'Aren't you asleep yet?'

'Where were you?'

'Up at Kathleen's.'

'Oh.'

Brendan took off his shoes and put them side by side on the floor below the bed.

'That's a girl.'

He shook his trousers carefully and hung them over the end of the bed.

'A great girl.'

'Did you tell her?'

'Tell her what?'

'About the . . . you know . . .'

'God, did I tell her? No way did I tell her.'

'I just thought you might have.'

He got into bed and pulled the clothes tight up around his chin.

'Good night.'

'Good night.'

'I might go back to England.'

'Oh.'

'Anyway, you keep your mouth shut.'

'Yeah.'

'Good night.'

'Good night.'

'And thanks.'

She was waiting for him the next afternoon, puffing away as usual. Her hair hung down her back like one of the young ones. She waved when she saw him coming. That made him feel good.

'How lovely.'

'What's lovely? To see you is lovely.'

He laughed.

'Come and have tea. Toasted sticky buns.'

'Yes.'

'I love toasted sticky buns.'

They crossed the road and he kept his feet pacing along beside hers, stretching his stride to keep her rhythm.

'Did you have a terrible time the other night?'

'They made an awful mess.'

'Your poor mother.'

'The whole street really . . . a terrible mess.'

'Were you scared?'

He thought of the gun.

'Oh, no. Not really . . . well . . .'

She laughed.

'I would have been. We must have another day at the sea. I enjoyed that, didn't you?'

'Or Grianan.'

'Or Grianan. Somewhere.'

'How's Fred Burgess?'

She looked surprised at the question.

'He's all right.'

'Does he write to you all the time?'

'He's not too bad.'

'And do you write to him?'

'Curiosity killed the cat.'

'But, do you?'

'I do.'

'Every day?'

'Don't be silly. Only Victorian ladies with nothing else to do were able to write letters every day to their gentlemen friends.'

'What would you say?'

'Dear sir, when I got up this morning at eight-fifteen it was, as usual, raining. I went to the bathroom and brushed my teeth thirty-seven times . . .'

'What sort of toothpaste do you use?'

'He would know. I'd have told him that already.'

'But you should do it. Then he would know everything about you.'

'Imagine how bored you'd get reading a letter like that, on and on. As long as a day itself and then knowing that another one would be coming tomorrow.'

'Your thoughts then. You could write him your thoughts.'

'Dear Joe, my thoughts are as boring as buying toothpaste.'

'I don't think so.'

'You're one of the nice people in the world.'

'Do I bore you?'

'Never.'

'Does Brendan bore you?'

She threw the remains of her cigarette into the gutter.

'What a strange thing to ask. No, I suppose. I hardly know him. He's in a state of great confusion. That always appeals to me.'

'Confusion?'

'Tangled up somehow. A lot of the wrong ideas pushing the right ideas rather hard. You don't like him much, do you?'

Joe blushed.

'He's O.K.'

She laughed.

'In ten years you'll feel differently. Confusion is hard for people of your age to understand.'

'Is Fred Burgess confused?'

'Absolutely.'

'Oh.' She took his arm and squeezed it tight up close to her side.

'Brendan might go away soon . . . I think . . . I hope . . he ought to go . . . really.'

From far away there was a burst of gunfire.

'Oh dear,' she said. She took a cigarette packet out of her pocket and looked at it.

'I think he'll go. It would be better. You know, I think I'm going to give it up.'

'That's good.'

She threw the box into the middle of the road

'There.'

'How many were in it?'

'Cheeky.'

She began to run, dragging him along with her.

'Quick, sticky buns.'

At her steps she stopped.

'I really mean it. I've had my last stick of poison.'

'I give you twenty-four hours.'

'Your windows are dirty.'

She was lighting matches in an abstracted way and the gas kept popping.

'There must be air in the pipes,' he said.

She put the matches down and came over to the window.

'I don't really look out much, so it doesn't worry me if they're clean or dirty. There's not much to see anyway.'

'No.'

'I suppose when those houses fall down they'll put up a huge tower block and I wouldn't want to look at that either.'

'You won't be here.'

She sighed and went back to the gas. This time it lit at once. He watched her quick neat fingers as she cut the buns and laid them on the griller and wondered if, in his life, he would ever meet anyone like her again.

'Are you all right?' she asked him.

'Yes. Why?'

'You don't look well.'

'I'm tired, I suppose.'

'All the kids are tired. It's been long.'

'What?'

'Oh, the winter perhaps.'

'What makes you think that Brendan will go?'

'Just a feeling I have. I don't know anything.' She looked rather fiercely at him. 'Nothing. It's best to know nothing. All or nothing. Otherwise you start making idiotic moral judgements. So I know nothing. I think he'll go away. He's not very strong. I don't mean Tarzan-strong. No strength inside. His mind is too open to suggestion. He needs a good friend.'

'You?'

She took one of the buns from under the grill and began to butter it.

'There's a lovely shop in Dublin makes the best sticky buns in the world. Bewleys. A great dark place. They sell coffee beans . . .' She lost the thread of her own words.

'Bewleys . . . ?'

She arranged the buns in a circle on a plate.

'Here.'

He took one from her. She stood looking down at him.

'Joe . . .'

The door behind her opened and Brendan came in, as if, thought Joe, he owned the place.

'The door below was open, so I came up.'

'You're just in time for a bun.'

'Hello, Joe.'

'Hello,' said Joe, his voice ungracious.

Brendan took a bun from the plate and the three of them stared at each other in silence.

'Tea anyone?' asked Kathleen eventually.

'Yes, please.' Both boys answered simultaneously.

'Are you glad to see me?' He put his head back like Dad did sometimes and laughed.

'Of course we're glad to see you.' She was pouring tea as she spoke. Without waiting to be asked Brendan took another bun from the plate. Like he owned the place. Joe chewed. Kathleen put two spoonfuls of sugar into a cup and handed it to Brendan. He didn't even say thanks

'Mam will be wondering where you are.'

'No, she won't.'

'She likes you to go straight home.'

'Not now the evenings are getting lighter. She doesn't mind.'

Kathleen handed him his tea.

'Thank you,' he said in a loud voice.

'If you two are going to fight,' she said, 'you must go and do it somewhere else.'

Silence.

'I'm sorry,' said Brendan. 'It's not my day. You're a great skin, Joe. I mean that.'

'Let's all be jolly.' Kathleen switched on the radio and there was a blast of music.

'No.'

178

'No.' She switched it off.

'Kathleen, I've got to talk to you.'

'Later . . .'

'Please.'

Joe got up. He still had half the bun in his hand.

'I've got to go.'

'Ah, Joe . . .'

'He's right about Mam.'

'I'm sorry, pet.'

'That's all right.'

She put her arms round him and kissed him.

'Tomorrow.'

Her face was soft and smelt of soap. He leaned against her cheek for a moment.

'Yes.'

'Everything will be all right tomorow. You'll see.'

He went down the stairs on his own, listening to their voices fade, and out into the street, still holding the bun. He dropped it in the gutter. He wondered what it was that Brendan wanted to say. He wondered why it was so hard to speak to people. When you were alone conversation thrived inside your head, but when confronted with another human being, even your thoughts died. A wind was scattering dust and papers round the street, feeling at his face with cold fingers. Would he tell her about the gun? What, anyway, about the gun? Had he ever used the gun? On the pictures they could look down the barrel and tell you. No one would ever know now. Unless, of course, they dragged the river. But they wouldn't. They wouldn't do that. A laughable thought. Was Brendan soft on her? It didn't really matter. She had Fred Burgess. The sooner she went away and married him the better.

Words run
In and out of your mind
Like children playing.
And then
When you really need them,

Like children,
They disappear.
Maybe tomorrow would be a good day. Maybe . . . maybe
. . . He was home.

No one was speaking that evening. His mother put the
food on the table and they ate in silence. Dad read the paper
and coughed from time to time. He ate nothing. His face
was pale and small beads of sweat gathered on his forehead
and clung to the sides of his nose. Brendan didn't appear.
Mam sighed and glanced at the clock from time to time.
His food dried in the oven. Joe did his homework and went
to bed.

The next morning he got up when he heard his mother
going down the stairs. He got dressed quickly and had his
hand on the door when Brendan spoke.
    'Joe.'
    'Yes.'
    'Tell Mam I'll be down soon for breakfast.'
    'You're early.'
    'I'm packing in the job.'
He sounded as if he were trying out the words for the
first time.
    'Oh.'
    'You don't sound surprised.'
    'What'll you do?'
He went over to the bed and looked down at his brother.
It always seemed strange to him that people who had been
asleep always smelt differently to those who had been up
and walking round a while.
    'Do for money, I mean.'
    'Money.' Brendan laughed.
    'Mam . . .'
    'Don't you say a word to her. Do you hear? I'll tell her
in my own way. In my own time . . . and him.'
    'Why?'

'I hadn't worked it out . . . you know, to the end. I can't explain . . . it's not even very clear to me, I always saw myself carrying on where he left off . . .'

'He? You mean Dad?'

'Yes. Yes. It was all like some sort of dream. Then when they gave me a gun . . . I was not the right person any more. I've gone ahead with it . . . only now . . . It was the gun finished me off. I wouldn't be any use to them . . . to anyone really . . . I feel wrecked. Jesus.'

'What'll you do?'

'Get out. Go back. I hate that . . . but . . . Get a job. Keep my mouth shut.'

'Kathleen . . .'

'Yes?'

'That's a great girl. A girl . . .'

The bed in the next room creaked under the movement of their father. The boys listened in silence for a moment.

'I told her everything.' Brendan whispered so softly that Joe had to lean forward to catch his words. She didn't want to know, a voice was crying in his head.

'She . . . she's . . . kind . . .'

'What did you tell her?'

'Never you mind, kiddo, what I told her. She listened. I've never met a girl like her before.'

Brendan smiled to himself.

'I'm just telling you because you were great, and I wouldn't want to go without saying anything. She said . . .'

'Go?'

'Aye. I'll go maybe today. She's lending me a few pounds till I get started.'

'Oh.'

'I don't want any fuss . . . so don't . . .'

'No.'

'She'll be over at the end of July. We'll maybe . . . I'd like . . . You never know what might happen . . . I'll get a decent job.'

'What are you talking about?'

'Don't be thick. We might get married.'

Joe heard his own voice coming out, cold and ugly.

'She's going to be married to someone else.'

Brendan laughed.

'Where did you get that bit of news?'

'She told me so herself. She doesn't tell you everything, so she doesn't.'

'You're a bit gone on her yourself.'

'I am not gone on her, but I can tell you something . . . she's not gone on you. She thinks you're weak. She told me so. She's going to be married to someone anyway. She loves him. She doesn't talk to you. She didn't even want to listen to you. She told me that too.'

Brendan threw back the clothes and put his feet down on the floor.

'You're a liar.'

Joe took a step backwards, away from him.

'I am not. Ask her. That's all you have to do. Ask her.'

'Is anything wrong up there?'

An anxious voice from the bottom of the stairs.

Brendan was coming across the floor after him, his bare feet squeaking on the lino.

He reached out and grabbed Joe by the back of the neck

'Lying little shite.'

and began shaking him.

'Boys. Brendan. Joe.'

Her footsteps started on the stairs.

'It's all right, Mam,' called Brendan. The footsteps stopped.

'I even know his name. She loved him yesterday. She talked about him yesterday. She writes him letters telling him everything.'

Brendan hit him across the face with the palm of his hand.

'Everything.'

Slap.

'Mammy, he's hitting me.'

'For the love of God.'

The door banged open and she stood looking at them.

'Brendan. Leave the child alone.'

'I'll leave him alone when I've finished with him.'

'What's he done to you?'

Her face was distracted.

'He's a bloody little liar.'

'Fred Burgess is his name.'

He wriggled out of Brendan's grip and dashed behind his mother.

'F.R.E.D.'

'Will ye shut up and give a man a chance to sleep?' A roar came from Dad's room.

Brendan made a grab at Joe.

'Burgess. Do you want me to spell that too?'

'Brendan. I don't know what it's all about . . .' She put out both her arms to stop him.

'And he's a soldier.'

Brendan stood quite still and looked at him.

'Liar.' He said the word uncertainly.

'Joe,' begged Mam.

There was nothing stopping him now though.

'A British soldier. She wears a ring, you know. And she tells him everything.'

He stepped cautiously on to the top step.

'Wait,' he said with madness in his voice, 'till she tells him what you told her last night.'

He was away off down the stairs. He pulled his anorak off the hook and opened the hall door.

'Ask her,' he shouted over his shoulder as he ran up the street. Curtains twitched with curiosity. He needn't have bothered running, Brendan never moved.

Joe ran for a long time without realising where he was going. His heart was hammering so hard inside him that it felt no longer as if it were in his chest, but as if it had escaped and was thudding in his legs and his head, even his hands felt as if they were going to burst. Gradually he slowed down to a walk and his heart returned to the correct position in his body. His head ached. He had an amazing thirst.

He found himself on the road that runs out along the river towards the border. The city was behind him. The high warehouses were behind him and the bombed-out shops, 'business as usual', scrawled bravely on the doors. He passed the bus depot and the army barracks and the neat houses with their front gardens rimmed with raked flower beds. The wind blew aimless seagulls across the sky and the river moved, silver, towards the lough. Nothing could stop that. Then it was country, and high trees leant in winter loneliness against the tumbling walls of the big houses. Cattle searched in the fields for grass. The bare hills came closer with every step he took.

What have I done? Deliberate destruction. I hated him. Only because . . . for some nameless reason. Some reason I don't understand. Father, I have sinned. Who will forgive me now? I have told the truth, but only to destroy. I too am destroyed. So forever is the destroyer destroyed. So . . .

'Everything will be all right tomorrow.'

Her voice was so gentle, and now she too would hate him. Worse, despise him.

A road to the right wandered down the hill towards the river. He went with it. Smoke streamed from the high chimneys of the power station on the other bank of the river. A curve of grey and white houses formed a bay, and boats rocked gently on its sheltered water. He sat down on a wall and looked at it all. Beyond the houses the river opened out wide into the lough and then somewhere far away there was the sea. The world. The real world. Perhaps it was all the same. Perhaps everywhere you went people were lost, searching with desperation for something they would never find. Mutilating themselves and each other in their desperation. There was no safety. A bird got up slowly from the field below him, ungainly for a moment and then soaring with a perfection that took away your breath. The song he had heard in her room came into his head.

I see the last black swan
Fly past the sun,

I wish I too were gone
Back home again.
My body's black and sore.
I need to sleep.
Now hear the heavens roar.
I can't escape.

Now we have time to kill . . .

A ship moved across the deep water of the tiny bay. The patterns in the water spread behind it like a peacock's tail.

Kill the shadows on our skin.

He could go home now. He slithered down from the wall, scraping the back of his right hand against the stone. He just had to go back.

Kill the fire that burns within.

It would only be a temporary measure. Killing time, my friend. Until such time. His behind was wet. Brendan would half-kill him, but then he was going away. Everything would be the way it was before then. Well . . .

Only a temporary measure. It was the shadows that hid the truth. The shadows . . . fearful. His legs were stiff with the unaccustomed walking and the dampness soaking through his trousers. She would understand. She would forgive him. She . . . He was hungry now. Mam would half-kill him for not having gone to school. If he was half-killed by Brendan and half-killed by Mam it didn't leave much of Joe. Ah well . . .

She didn't even ask him where he'd been. She indicated his chair. He sat down. His back ached. He wasn't cut out for the energetic life.

'Let there be no more fighting,' she said, putting his plate down in front of him. 'Your Daddy is ill with it all. Lying up there moaning and groaning as if his last hour had come.'

There was no sign of Brendan that evening, nor was he in his bed when Joe got up the next morning.

'Where's Brendan?'

'Is he not in his bed?'

'No.'

'He must be working so. He said nothing to me. He was in a wild state yesterday and he leaving the house.'

She laughed, for some reason of her own.

'You shouldn't have said those things to him. I thought he was going to kill you.'

'So did I.'

They both laughed. How odd that they should be sitting there laughing. Odd. She didn't know just how odd.

'Who was this girl anyway?' She was still smiling as she asked the question.

'A girl he knew. A teacher . . . don't remember her name.'

He shook some corn flakes into his bowl. The laughter had left him now. He didn't want her questions.

'Was it true what you said about her?'

'I heard it around.'

'Was it true?'

'How would I know? He annoyed me, so I said it.'

'If only you wouldn't fight.'

He hurried through his breakfast, hoping to get away before she started again.

'You shouldn't say things like that if they're not true.'

'Maybe it's true.'

Mam frowned.

'I'd like to get her for messing around with Brendan.'

'Ah, Mam . . .'

'I would.'

He got up.

'I'd better go.'

'Aye. Run on, son. Be sure you're back in time to bring your Daddy up his cup of tea. You've been wild lately . . .'

'All right, Mam.'

'I hear Brendan's away again.'

Peter was waiting for him outside the school gate.

'Where did you hear that?'

'Everyone has it.'

'I wouldn't know.'

'What do you mean?'

'I haven't seen him since yesterday morning.'

'Where were you yesterday anyway?'

'I was sick.'

'Mauryah.'

'It's true.'

'He's gone. He got in trouble with the boys and he's gone. Isn't it a funny thing he didn't tell you.'

'I suppose he didn't want to worry Mam.'

'Everyone has it.'

'So you said.' _

'I wouldn't like to get in trouble with the boys. They can follow you to the ends of the earth.'

'Ah, shut up.'

'What do you think he did?'

'I haven't a clue.'

'Do you think he informed?'

'Do you want your teeth bashed in?'

'Try it.'

They scuffled in a half-hearted way until the bell rang.

God the Father, maker of Heaven and earth let him be gone.

Lamb of God who takest away the sins of the world, let him be gone.

Holy Mary, Mother of God, let him be gone. Amen.

That litany was all that he had in his head. No one bothered him all morning. The teachers must have been aware that he had troubles, because they left him alone. No one enquired about his exercises, nor did they ask him to speak in class.

He wondered how God managed to hear everyone's prayers, or did he have a secretary who passed on the most important ones, and who was to judge anyway? I will do my homework for the rest of the year. I will listen in class. I will kneel on the cold lino every night to say my prayers . . . he thought of the empty promises he had already made and given up. Miss McCabe drew a map of Ireland on the black-board. Squeak went the chalk. One by one she called the boys up to fill in the names of the towns and rivers. Mr Harkin's voice droned through the wall, like a bee on a summer day. A helicopter clattered past.

I will see her after school. I will explain. Everything will be all right. She will understand.

Peter nudged him. The class was over.

'Wake up.'

Joe grabbed at his books and shoved them into his satchel. He heard Peter's voice speaking. He would go now. He would wait there on the step till she came home. He would tell her everything. He would tell her he was sorry. Now . . . He ran out of the classroom.

'Hey . . .' called Peter.

There was a woman on the doorstep of Kathleen's house.

'Excuse me . . .' he said.

She didn't move out of his way. She wore fluffy slippers like Mam's and a flowered apron over her jumper and skirt. She was smoking.

'Excuse me . . .'

She took the cigarette out of her mouth.

'Have you come to see her?'

A jerk of the head up towards the window.

'Yes.'

'I thought I'd seen you here before. You're only just in time.'

'In time?' His heart bumped.

'She's getting out.'

'Out?'

'That's what I said.'

'But . . .?'

'I know nothing. I don't care. Just as long as she gets out.'

She moved slightly to one side to let him pass. He ran up the stairs and knocked on Kathleen's door.

'Who is it?'

188

'Joe.'

He heard her walk across the room and unlock the door. She opened it slowly and stood looking at him.

'Yes,' she said. Her voice was cold. 'What do you want?'

He wouldn't have recognised her if he'd seen her in the street. Except for her clothes. He'd have known them. Her hair had been cut short like a man's. Her face was swollen. One of her eyes was almost closed.

'What . . . what's the matter? What's happened? How . . .?'

'Don't you know?'

'Kathleen . . . What's happened? Your face. Why are you going away?'

'Your brother has nice friends.'

He started to cry. Huge, hot tears rushed up through his entire body and burst out of his eyes.

'I . . . I . . . I . . .'

She looked at him helplessly for a moment.

'Come in.'

She shut and locked the door behind them. Two cases waited on the floor and a third was still open on the bed.

'I have to catch the Dublin bus.'

'But . . .'

She began to pack books into the top of the case. Her back was to Joe, her movements quick and neat, as always.

'I'm only bringing my clothes and books. I don't want anything else. I don't want to see or touch any of these things again. I've thrown out all the clothes I was wearing yesterday when they . . . when . . . if I'd the money, I'd throw out everything I owned yesterday. Everything. Here.' She picked up a book from the bed and handed it to him. 'I've always meant to give you that.'

'Kathleen . . .'

'I didn't want you to come. I wanted to go away from here hating everyone very much.'

'I came to say I'm sorry. Please don't go . . . please. I'm sorry. I'm sorry.'

She shut the lid of the case and turned and looked at him. On the table beside her an ashtray was full of butts.

'Why did you do it? You?'

Her voice was almost casual, almost unconcerned. Without waiting for him to answer, she turned back to the case and began to struggle with the catch. He wanted to tell her that he had done it because he loved her, but he didn't know how to. He continued to cry. With a click the case was shut. She lifted it down on to the floor. A car outside blew its horn.

'That's my taxi.'

She picked up her coat from the bed and put it on.

'Where are you going?'

'Away.'

She tied a large red scarf around her head. The car hooted again.

'I must go, Joe. Will you help me carry the cases down? Here.'

She pushed a large white handkerchief into his hand. He wiped his face and blew his nose. She unlocked the door.

'I don't want you to go. Was it all . . . all my fault?'

She smiled at him suddenly and put out her hand as she used to do and touched his face.

'Poor Joe. I don't suppose it was. One day we'll see . . . one day we'll forget it all. One day . . .'

She handed him a case and he thought of Brendan and the time, the first time, he had gone down the hill, leaning over with the weight of the case in his hand. They bumped down the stairs. The woman was still there, determined to see them off the premises.

She slammed the door viciously behind them when they were on the step.

Kathleen suddenly grinned at Joe as she put the cases on the ground. The driver got out of the car and put the luggage in the boot.

'Anyway,' she said. 'You were right. I'm back on the poison again.'

'I'm sorry, Kathleen. I'm sorry. If . . .'

She kissed him. Her face was hot to touch. She got quickly into the car.

'If ifs and ans were pots and pans . . .'

She closed the door and lifted a thin white hand in farewell. He stood on the pavement and watched the car until it was out of sight, then he looked at the red book which he held in his right hand. It was called *A Golden Treasury of Verse*. He opened it and looked at what she had written in childish writing on the first page.

Kathleen Doherty is my name,
Ireland is my nation,
Wicklow is my dwelling place,
And heaven my destination.

He looked down the street but the taxi was truly gone. Carefully, he put the book into his pocket and started off home to get his father a cup of tea.